SARAH

TERI POLEN

BLACK ROSE
writing™

The final approval for this literary material is granted by the author.

First printing

This is a work of fiction. Names, characters, businesses, places, events and incidents are either the products of the author's imagination or used in a fictitious manner. Any resemblance to actual persons, living or dead, or actual events is purely coincidental.

ISBN: 978-1-61296-791-2
PUBLISHED BY BLACK ROSE WRITING
www.blackrosewriting.com

Printed in the United States of America
Suggested retail price $17.95

Sarah is printed in Minion Pro

To my Dad, who passed on to me his love of reading and allowed me as a little girl to stay up late with him and watch Chiller Theatre, forever warping my impressionable young mind. Looks like it paid off.

SARAH

SARAH

CHAPTER 1

I might as well have been a ghost. Standing in front of the department store mirror as Erin fussed about me, tugging at the sleeves and bottom of the shirt she'd forced me to try on, I caught the reflection of two girls from my chemistry class giggling and whispering to each other as they enjoyed my obvious discomfort.

"What was wrong with the shirt I chose? I liked it better." She stared at the combination of clothes I was wearing, but didn't see me. Not really. "Erin?" I tried again. Yep – I was a ghost. She couldn't hear me either. So I waited, thinking about all the other places I'd rather be.

"Cain, your wardrobe consists of hoodies, sports jerseys, and t-shirts. No one would ever confuse you with a fashion mogul. I think you should try something different, a new look," she said, crossing her arms over her chest and frowning. "This one isn't working. Stay here and I'll get something else for you."

"I can't wait," I sighed. Erin and I had been together for the past three months. My dating experience was practically nonexistent and consisted of groups of friends going to movies, parties - stuff like that. Girls were like a foreign country to me and I didn't speak the language. The few times I'd asked someone out had ended in soul-crushing rejection or dates filled with long spans of awkward silences because I never knew what to say.

Erin was one of those girls everyone noticed – she was a cheerleader and always seemed to look perfect, never a hair out of place or chipped nail polish. Not that I knew anything about fashion, which apparently was the reason I was being held against my will at Rue 21, but I'd heard other girls talk about how much they loved the way Erin dressed. Yeah, she was hot, but someone I'd always considered out of my league.

So when she began talking to me at a party, then showed up at my soccer game the next week and started hanging around my locker at school, shocked didn't begin to explain how I'd felt. I couldn't say exactly when it happened, but all of a sudden, I had a girlfriend.

"Here, take these and try them on. Make sure to come out so I can see how they look," she said, layering my arms with five shirts I had no interest in wearing.

"We've only got forty-five minutes before the movie starts, so how about picking out the two you like best."

"Movie?" she asked, digging through her purse and pulling out a tube of lip gloss. "Oh, right. I didn't want to see that stupid horror movie anyway, so I told Ashley and Nick we'd meet them at Blue Finn for dinner."

"But you know I've been waiting all summer for this movie to come out and we'd planned to see it opening night."

"Maybe we can get to it sometime this weekend," she said, admiring herself in the mirror and flipping her hair over her shoulder. "Now hurry and get in the dressing room. I don't want to be late."

"Fine," I said, clenching my jaw. "But why are we going to Blue Finn? You know I don't like sushi."

"Cain, you know it's my favorite. I'm sure you can find something on the menu," Erin said, flashing me the smile that used to make me light-headed, but I now knew was as fake as her nails.

The first couple of months with Erin had been incredible and I couldn't believe she'd chosen to be with a guy like me. But lately, not so incredible. I'd thought we had a lot in common - turns out that was Erin's game. She lured guys in with her looks and the pretense of shared interests, then when they were hooked, she real Erin was unleashed. And she was not pretty. As my best friend said, she's beautiful from a distance. Up close, not so much. He'd also pointed out her interest in me began around the same time I was named soccer captain for the upcoming season. By some ridiculous social hierarchy rules I was unaware of, dating athletes was a plus. Dating team captains was a bigger bonus. Seriously, who made up these things?

For two weeks now, I'd been wanting to break up with Erin, but had no idea how to do it or what to say. Some couples broke up by text, but I wasn't that harsh. Erin was a bit of a drama queen at times, creating very public scenes when things didn't go her way. Like earlier in the summer when we'd gone to the beach and another girl was wearing the same swimsuit. Erin could have just laughed it off, but instead made loud, body-shaming comments about the poor girl, who was embarrassed enough to leave after fifteen minutes. I was mortified, being more of a 'fly under the radar' kind of guy.

So, here I was, miserable and fearful of the reaction of the most self-absorbed mean girl I'd ever known - if I found a way to end our relationship.

"Awesome. Ashley and Nick – sushi at Blue Finn." If shopping at Citadel Mall wasn't bad enough, now I was having dinner with Ashley, whose shrill voice matched the pitch of a dentist's drill, and Nick, who was shallower than a kiddie pool, and had a constant vacant look on his face. Sometimes I wondered how he found his way home at night.

Perfect ending to a perfect evening.

. . . . .

All through dinner, I kept thinking how I'd rather have been tied to a chair, eyes taped open, and forced to watch a marathon of the Kardashians than spend time with Erin and her friends. It was highly possible it would have been more intellectually stimulating.

"Mom, I'm home," I called, opening the door that led from the garage to the laundry room. Rounding the corner to the kitchen, I found my best friend, Finn, sweaty, smelly, and in need of a shower, sitting at the counter while my mom loaded his plate with chocolate chip cookies. "So I'm gone for a few hours and you get a new son?"

Mom kissed my cheek, and placed a plate of cookies in front of me as I took a seat beside Finn. "Don't be silly, sweetie, you know I'd never replace you. Finn came over to do the mowing and trimming."

"You didn't have to ask Finn, I told you I'd do it this weekend."

"You've been busy around here all week cleaning out the garage and making repairs. I wanted you to go out with Erin and have some fun. Besides, Finn offered a few days ago to work for cookies."

I glanced over at Finn as he grinned at me, teeth riddled with chocolate, enough to make me lose my appetite - but not quite. It's chocolate. Enough said.

Since my Dad had died in a car accident last year, a lot of responsibilities had fallen to me. Not that I minded, but sometimes I felt guilty if I wasn't here when Mom needed me for something. Finn McLachlan had been my best friend since second grade when we'd met on a soccer team, so we'd practically grown up together. My parents used to joke that he was their bonus son since he spent so much time at our house, especially when his parents went through a pretty nasty divorce a few years back. My Mom had given him a key and told him to use it whenever he needed to come over and spend the night or just get away from home for a while. And Finn had taken her up on it. There had been plenty of mornings I'd awakened to find him sprawled across the futon in my bedroom after letting himself into the house during the early morning hours, tired of listening to his parents' screaming matches.

When we'd moved to this smaller house after my Dad died, Mom had given keys to me, my sister Maddie, and Finn, saying each family member needed their own. With my Dad gone, Finn helped with the lawn, minor repairs around the house, errands and babysitting Maddie. He did this because to him, we're his family. It was comforting to know if I couldn't be here, Finn had my back.

"The words Erin and fun are incompatible in a sentence and should never be combined," Finn said, thankfully washing the cookies down with milk before speaking. "That girl could suck the fun out of Disney World and if your son would grow a set, Mrs. Shannon, maybe he'd take me up on my offer to blindfold her, drive her out to the middle of nowhere and turn her loose in the wild. Cain's quality of life would be kicked up several notches."

Mom leaned against the counter, reached across and tucked a strand of my hair behind my ear. "Cain, if you don't care about Erin, it isn't fair to keep stringing her along."

"In his defense, Mrs. Shannon, it's Erin that's stringing Cain along. She has a history of dating athletes, and with his total lack of experience with girls, Erin probably figured Cain was putty in her hands, ready to be molded to her liking."

"You know I can hear you, right?" I asked, shooting a sideways glare at Finn. "I want to break up with her, Mom. She makes me completely miserable, but I'm afraid of hurting her feelings. What if she cries? I have no idea what to do with crying women."

"You're assuming she has feelings?" Finn asked. "The few times I've had to talk to her, I decided your cat crushes Erin's score on the emotional IQ scale. Get rid of her, bro."

"I will. Just quit nagging me about it," I snapped.

"Then quit whining about her."

Mom gathered our empty plates, even the melted chocolate that had dripped from the cookies finger swiped and eaten. "Well, boys, I'll just leave you to figure it out for yourselves. I'm going to make sure Maddie is actually sleeping and not sneaking and reading books again. Are you staying over, Finn?"

"Naw, we'll probably play a little PS4 for a while then I'll head on home. My dad's out with someone he met on one of those dating websites I convinced him to try, so I kind of want to see how it went."

"Well, good for him," Mom said, patting Finn's arm. "I hope it goes well. Goodnight, boys." After standing on her tiptoes to kiss us both on the forehead, she walked down the hall toward her and Maddie's bedrooms.

. . . . .

My bedroom was on the opposite side of the house from the others, so my late hours of gaming and trash talking with Finn didn't keep anyone awake. As we walked into the room, Eby, my black cat, stretched and rolled over on my bed, lazily opening one green eye to stare at us.

"Dude, you might want to consider putting Eby on a weight program. How much are you feeding him?"

"He's not fat, just a little over-fluffy, and he can understand everything you're saying, so shut up." Eby was now sitting up, fully awake, staring intently at Finn with a superior expression on his face. Now that I thought about it, that was Eby's usual demeanor. Didn't most cats consider themselves superior to humans?

Finn and I took our usual spots in the gaming chairs in front of the TV. While I put in Destiny, my newest PS4 game, he picked up a half empty bag of barbecue potato chips from the floor and began munching. That's the good thing about my room. If the zombie apocalypse happened tomorrow, I could survive for at least a month on the partial bottles of Gatorade and water, protein bars, chips, trail mix, and beef jerky littering the majority of horizontal spaces in my room. Mom called me a pig. I preferred the term survivalist.

We played for a while and talked strategy for the upcoming soccer game on Saturday, while Eby stalked Finn, leaping across his lap occasionally just to keep him on his toes.

"Told you not to make that remark about his weight. If he goes into stealth mode, you'll never see the attack coming."

"So, you're saying I should apologize to your cat," Finn scoffed.

"How long have you known Eby? If you ever want to sleep peacefully again when you're here, I'd strongly consider it. Just saying." Out of the corner of my eye, I saw movement, but didn't pay much attention, figuring it was just Eby nosing around the room. The next thing I knew, he hissed, let out a screeching yowl, and scrambled out of the room faster than the speed of sound, while Finn yelped in surprise, tossing his controller into the air as Eby leapt over him.

"Cain, what's wrong with your cat? I think he just tried to kill me."

"You're still alive aren't you? So stop complaining."

Finn picked up his controller again, mumbling something about catnip and hallucinogens, and we continued playing, traversing the surface of Jupiter.

"Where's that cold air coming from?" Finn asked.

"Dude, we live in Charleston, the most humid city in South Carolina, where air conditioners keel over and die every few years."

"I know what the air conditioner feels like, and this ain't it." Turning in my direction, Finn's gaze focused on something over my head. "Why is the attic door open?"

Looking over my shoulder, I saw the wide open doorway, the light from the lamp on my nightstand forcing the darkness away from the first few stairs. The access door to the attic was in my room, but it was a normal-sized door, not the kind that pulled down from the ceiling. When we'd moved into this house, it made the job of lugging boxes upstairs a lot easier.

"That's weird," I said, frowning. "I know it wasn't open when we came in. We would have noticed it and Eby would have sprinted upstairs to explore."

"What's even weirder is the frigid arctic air coming down the stairs from your un-air-conditioned attic in mid-September. The temperature up there should at least be in the nineties."

Finn was right. There was no air conditioning in the attic and I also felt an icy draft coming through the door. "Well, if I'm going up there to check it out, you're coming with me," I said, rolling out of the gamer chair to a standing position.

"Fine. But if we see any spiders, you're on your own."

I flicked the switch on the wall inside the attic door and the light at the top of the stairs came on. Gazing up, I halfway expected to see snow flurries, the air was so cold. I rubbed my hands briskly over the growing goosebumps on my arms and noticed Finn doing the same.

We both trekked up the stairs, our feet landing heavily, probably loud enough to wake my Mom. I wondered if it was a subconscious attempt to scare away anyone – or anything – that might be lurking in the attic waiting for us. My imagination was vivid and I loved my horror movies and books, but I really didn't think there was anything supernatural about the cold air flowing down from the attic. But it was fun to think about.

As we reached the top of the stairs, I turned on the second switch, and dim light chased away the shadows in the storage area. Surveying the room, I saw it was just as Finn and I had left it in June when we'd moved in. Boxes full of holiday decorations, old baby clothes, some of my Dad's belongings, and soccer trophies were stacked neatly on the floor. Nothing out of the ordinary. No one waiting with an axe.

I'd nearly forgotten about Finn standing behind me and when he placed his hand on my shoulder, I bit back a yelp. "Maybe the air conditioning ducts are screwed up. You never know about the quality of work with these newer houses, they build them so fast. It might be pressure from within the house, you know, open one door and somewhere else in the house another one closes. Kind of like the laundry room door at my house when someone opens the back door."

"I'd think that was a possibility if there were any ducts in this room or if my bedroom door was open."

Finn stepped from behind me and crept slowly around the room, squinting into the dark, dusty corners and inspecting areas behind the boxes. "Maybe you should have someone come and check it out."

"Yeah, I guess I should mention it to Mom. Let's go back downstairs. We're not going to figure out anything tonight, and it's late." Finn didn't object and for that, I was relieved. I scanned the area once more before turning off the light, but still seeing nothing out of the ordinary, we went back downstairs. I didn't mention it to him because he'd never let me live it down, but the whole time we were in the attic, I'd had a creepy feeling someone was watching us, following our every movement. But that was impossible, of course.

CHAPTER 2

When the music alarm went off on my phone the next morning, my brain was a little fuzzy at first, but then I remembered what day it was. Today was Friday, which meant a pep rally for the soccer game tomorrow, and no calculus class today – could life get any better?

I rubbed my eyes and stretched, then swung my feet over the side of the bed and froze. The attic door was standing wide open again. I was positive I'd shut it last night after Finn and I came downstairs because the frigid air was turning my room into an igloo. And because the sensation of feeling like someone had been watching us was lingering and freaking me out a little. The air wafting down from the attic this morning was warm and humid like it should be in the middle of September.

Maybe whatever had happened last night was a fluke. Maybe the latch was loose and the door couldn't close completely. Whatever the case, I got up and shut the door firmly, tugging the knob to see if it would slip open, but the latch seemed solid. I shrugged and decided to check out the attic again after I got home from school. Maybe the feelings from last night wouldn't seem so realistic during daylight hours.

After showering, I went downstairs to feed Eby and grab some breakfast. Despite his actions toward Finn last night, Eby was a people lover and usually approved or disapproved all newcomers in our house. In hindsight, I should have taken his opinion of Erin into account long ago. The first time Erin came over, Eby jumped on the couch to greet her, sniffed her arm, scrunched up his black nose and hissed, then took a swing at her and fled the room. Erin's reaction to Eby was to move as far away from him as possible, saying he'd get black fur on her new jeggings, whatever those were. Since then, every time she'd come over Eby hissed at her and then disappeared, only returning after Erin was gone. I'd thought about making it a cardinal rule to never trust anyone who didn't like my cat, or have Eby approve any new girlfriends.

14

Assuming I'd actually get up the nerve to ask someone out – after I figured out how to dump Erin.

I walked into semi-controlled chaos. The kitchen was a hub of activity – Eby yowling for his breakfast, Mom packing lunches, eating yogurt, and signing field trip forms, and Maddie, my seven-year-old sister, attempting to put books in her backpack, papers trailing on the floor behind her.

"I've got two houses to show this evening, so you two are on your own tonight," Mom said, juggling the container of yogurt while she tossed a bag of carrots in Maddie's lunch bag. "Alright, lunches are made, taco meat is cooked and in the fridge, so I'll see you two tonight when I get home. Maddie, make sure to turn in your forms. Cain, are you sure you don't mind fixing dinner and helping Maddie with homework – again?"

"Mom, I got this. Don't worry," I said, grabbing a banana from the fruit bowl.

"I know it's not your responsibility to take care of her, Cain. You should be with your friends, or even on a date, not taking care of your sister."

I rolled my eyes. "Mom, believe me, I'd much rather be helping Maddie with second grade math and reading *Harry Potter* to her at bedtime than go out with Erin."

Her shoulders sagged in relief. "Thanks, sweetie. I know my hours have been kind of crazy lately, but I really appreciate you being here for Maddie. I know she's in good hands," she said, standing on her tiptoes to kiss my cheek.

"Maddie's no problem – a little weird, but fun in a warped kind of way." I watched as she alternated spooning cereal in her mouth then feeding Eby a spoonful of milk – with the same spoon.

"Were you planning to go out with Erin tonight?"

"That would be a no, I'm free from her clutches."

"Remember what I said about letting her know how you feel. It will only get worse if you drag it out."

"Working on it, Mom," I said, as I filled Eby's food bowl.

After watching ESPN and catching up on some scores, I went back upstairs to finish getting ready, Eby at my heels. While pulling back my hair with a leather tie, I noticed Eby nosing through the protein bar wrappers, chip bags, and empty glasses that littered my floor. He started batting around what looked like a red Skittle and knocked it under the attic door. Flopping over to his side, he stuck his paws under the door, trying to retrieve the red candy, but suddenly stiffened and pounced backwards, landing in a crouched position.

"What's your problem? Something grab your paw on the other side?" Eby's black fur was standing on end, his tail bushed out to twice its normal size, and I heard a low growl coming from his throat.

"Dorky cat. There's nothing there. I'll prove it to you," I said, opening the door. Eby sank back into the corner, his ears flat against his head as he hissed at the empty doorway. He then shot across the bed and out of my room, an almost identical reaction to last night. I again thought about the creepy feeling I'd had in the attic. Then I remembered my new rule of trusting Eby's reactions to people and wondered if this was another time I should trust his instincts.

Especially as unnaturally cold air wafted into the room through the open attic doorway, surrounding my body like an icy cocoon. I slammed the door, grabbed the chair from my desk, and jammed the back of it under the door knob. Surely that would keep the door closed. I hoped.

CHAPTER 3

While I was happy to miss calculus because of the pep rally, I was relieved it didn't interfere with English lit. This was the best part of my day. Not because of my love of all that was literature - I didn't know the difference between William Shakespeare and Stephen King. This was the best part of my day because of who else was in the class. And there she was, coming through the door.

Lindsey Sullivan. She and her brother, Caleb, who was also on the soccer team, had transferred to our school last year, but I'd only gotten to know her over the last month. The gods had been smiling down upon me when the alphabetical seating chart placed her beside me and since then we'd been talking some before and after class.

"Hey, Cain," she said, tucking her long blond hair behind one ear as she tossed her backpack onto the floor and took her seat. Wow, she always smelled so good, like a mixture of citrus and cinnamon, not that flowery crap Erin wore that always made me think of my grandma.

"Did you watch the Broncos game last night?" she asked, leaning over to tie her red Chucks. From this angle, I could see the curve of her neck and the glint of a silver chain as her hair fell forward. I imagined what it would be like to move my lips along the path of her neck up to just below her ear and.....

Snapping fingers in front of my face. "Cain? Are you with me?" she asked. I was so caught up in my daydream, I hadn't noticed Lindsey sitting up again.

"What? Sorry, Lindsey," I said, ducking my head, sure my face was the color of her Chucks. "I didn't get to watch the game last night, but saw the highlights on TV this morning."

"You missed a Broncos game?" her eyes widening in surprise. "What could keep you from that, 'cause I know soccer practice was over by five since I had to pick up Caleb."

"I was dragged to the mall against my will," I replied, twisting the silver ring I wore on my right index finger.

"Finn made you go shopping again? Isn't his closet overflowing with shoes by now?"

I snorted out loud, like the total babe magnet I was. "Yeah, I wish. Um, Erin needed to look for.... some kind of shirt or something. I really wasn't paying attention," I said, glancing sideways at her. Something flitted across her face, a girl look I was unfamiliar with. Sometimes I wished Maddie was older and could interpret things for me, explaining the foreign language of the female species. Life would be so much easier.

"Yeah, well that's what happens when you date those prom queen types. It's all fun and games until they need to go shopping."

"It's definitely not all fun and games," I muttered.

"What was that?" Lindsey asked, a definite smirk on her face. That look I knew.

"Nothing. You coming to the soccer game tomorrow?"

"Are you kidding? After what they did to us in regionals last season, I wouldn't miss this game for anything. I have orchestra practice in the morning, but I'll just toss the cello in the back of the Jeep and then a few of us plan to head over after that."

"Seriously? You'll just toss the cello in the Jeep. It's almost as big as you are," I chuckled.

"Hey, I can handle it," she huffed. "Why don't you come to our concert next week?" Wait – I think – yep. My heart stopped. Did Lindsey just ask me out? If I didn't know better, I'd say she even looked hopeful, but since I don't speak girl language, I was probably completely misinterpreting her expression.

"I..." Before I could finish, Mrs. Brody called the class to order, crushing my dream. Time to discuss *Gone With the Wind*. Perfect.

• • • • •

Plopping my lunch tray on the table, I pulled out the seat across from Finn. What could I say about the items on my tray? What horror stories about high school cafeterias haven't you heard? The lunch ladies were scary and intimidating and barked at the students like coarse, gruff military men and the food came in colors, textures, and smells that were indescribable and truly frightening, not to mention unappetizing. Most of the students had an irrational fear of being stabbed with sporks by the lunch ladies or developing food poisoning.

Gazing across the table, I grinned after reading Finn's choice of t-shirt today. It read, 'The Third Rule of Fight Club Is Have Fun and Try Your Best'. Most of his wardrobe consisted of t-shirts that were nerdy, humorous, or downright offensive, but always brought on a snort of laughter.

"Need your expertise, bro. If Lindsey asked me to come to her concert, does that count as a date or was she just being friendly?"

"Cain, my young, inexperienced Padawan, I sense the force isn't strong in you, but use your feelings you must."

I raised an eyebrow at him. "Seriously? You're going to quote *Star Wars* now?"

"When is it not an appropriate time to quote *Star Wars*? Words to live by, my friend."

"Still waiting."

"Fine. Dump Erin, go out with Lindsey. Sounds like she's into you, dude. She's not like that pack Erin runs with and I don't think shopping is high on her list of priorities. Lindsey's friends are like real people, not clones of each other. And another bonus – you can actually talk to her. An even bigger bonus is that she likes yours truly. Obviously, she has good taste."

"Obviously," I muttered, sporking some sort of reddish-colored lump on my tray.

Speak of the devil – and the angel, a long blond mane of hair caught my eye and Lindsey, catching me looking at her, turned and said something to her two friends, Ling and Emma, then waved and walked toward our table, carrying her lunch tray. Unfortunately, the devil herself, Erin, narrowed her eyes at Lindsey after seeing her wave and raced behind her in our direction.

Lindsey slid her lunch tray onto the table and took the seat to Finn's left. "Hey, Cain. 'Sup Finn. Sweet t-shirt – awesome movie, but the book was better."

Before I could say a word, Erin reached the table, leaned over and kissed me, then sat beside me, directly across from Lindsey. "Hi, baby, I missed you this morning. Finn," Erin said, barely glancing in his direction, but she definitely noticed Lindsey, pursing her lips as she placed her hand on my thigh. "Oh, Lisa, I didn't know you were Finn's wench of the week. That must be….interesting."

To her credit, Lindsey gave a bemused smile. "It's Lindsey, not Lisa, and no, I'm not with Finn but, with his wicked t-shirt collection, exquisite sense of humor, and Harry Potteresque chaotic hair, any girl would consider herself lucky to be his wench for a week."

"Can't argue with the truth," Finn said, beaming.

"Well, I consider myself a great judge of character," Lindsey said, looking directly at Erin. "I've always preferred to spend my time with people who are genuine and can think for themselves."

Erin glared at Lindsey, whose radiant smile clearly showed she was enjoying herself. I, however, was in pain because of the way Erin gripped my thigh, her long pink talons digging into my leg and probably leaving marks. Grabbing her hand, I pried it away, and dropped it in her lap. This didn't go over so well with Erin, as she whipped her head around, eyes blazing at me. Finn and Lindsey were both trying to hide their laughter while they picked at their food.

The rest of lunch break was spent with Erin giving me the cold shoulder, something I didn't mind, and Finn, Lindsey, and I talking about the soccer game tomorrow and Lindsey's upcoming concert.

After lunch, I hoped Erin's icy silent treatment would hold, but before we parted ways, she grabbed the back of my neck, pulled my head to hers and kissed me. She then gave Lindsey a cold scowl. "Oh, by the way, Lisa, nice shoes."

"Thanks, I've got three more like them at home. I'd give you the name of the store, but they're really selective about their clientele."

If the imaginary daggers spewing from Erin's eyes had been real, Lindsey would have bled out in front of us. Instead, Erin spun on her heel and caught up with a friend, leaving Lindsey laughing in her wake. "She's really, um…something, isn't she? See you guys later."

I watched Lindsey walk away from me down the hallway, imagining what it would have been like if she'd kissed me instead Erin. Why was I worried about hurting the feelings of someone who cared so little about my own?

. . . . .

When I got home after soccer practice that evening, I sprinted up the stairs to make sure the attic door was still closed. Before I entered my room, I noticed my legs seemed a little wobbly, but figured it was only because of the strenuous practice. Not because I was afraid the chair would be kicked over and the door wide open. That would be ridiculous.

Taking a deep breath, I crossed the threshold and looked to my left. Seeing the chair and door were just as I'd left them this morning, I let out the breath I'd been holding. Everything was fine. Whatever had happened last night and this morning had been a fluke with the ventilation system like Finn said. That was all. I chuckled, shaking my head at how Finn and I had reacted, then went in my bathroom to shower.

. . . . .

"Wingardium Leviosa!" Maddie waved her wand at me with flourish and a flick of her wrist. "Cain, why aren't you floating? That's what the spell is for, so float!"

"Sorry, Maddie. Maybe you need to practice on smaller things first. Like Eby."

With Mom out showing houses to clients, I'd reheated the taco meat she'd made this morning for dinner, helped Maddie with her homework, and supervised bath time. We were currently dueling each other with our wands. Her recent fascination with all things Harry Potter had led her to make her own wand from a tree twig she'd found in the backyard. My wand was a chopstick I'd discovered on my floor from when Finn and I had takeout Chinese earlier this week.

Even though Mom felt guilty about me taking care of Maddie so much, I hadn't been lying when I'd told her I didn't mind. She was a funny kid and with Dad being gone, I wanted to continue some of the things with Maddie they'd done together, and he'd always read to her before bedtime. We were on the third *Harry Potter* book and she was captivated. Promising to read to her also made it easier to get her settled in bed.

"Eby's going to Hogwarts with me when my letter comes, so I can't practice on him. I don't want to turn his hair pink or give him a pig's tail."

"Good point. Pink hair would ruin his street cred. How about we continue this duel tomorrow and start the next chapter?"

. . . . .

I turned in around midnight, Eby a warm, furry lump up at my side, while thoughts of tomorrow's game swirled in my head. Exhausted from the afternoon's practice and an evening with Maddie, I drifted off easily, my thoughts gliding to Lindsey from earlier today, and the vision of her curved neck with the silver chain. I imagined myself going to her concert and maybe doing something cheesy and romantic, like bringing her flowers after it was over.

Why was it so warm in here? Sometimes I was a little uncomfortable with Eby's body heat added to my own, but this was approaching sauna levels. Still half-asleep, something tickled at the back of my mind, but wasn't ready to become a conscious thought. I tried to shove the covers off me, but they were stuck on something. I reached for Eby to push him out of the way, but my hand came up empty. I didn't feel him beside me anywhere and my brow furrowed, thinking how strange that was. He usually stayed with me all night so he could wake me early for his breakfast. Too tired to think about it now, I at least managed to kick the covers off my legs up to my knees.

Falling deeper towards sleep, I sensed my hair being stroked back from my forehead with a cool hand and it felt wonderful against my heated skin. This was how Mom used to relax me after a nightmare when I was younger or couldn't sleep. She hadn't done this since I'd been sick with the flu a couple of years ago.

Except .....

Deep down my subconscious was screaming, telling me something was wrong. What was it?

I struggled to wake myself, frantically climbing toward consciousness as I brushed at my forehead, expecting to feel someone else's hands. Bolting straight up, fully awake now, I scrutinized the room, peering into the corners with their murky shadows. I fumbled across the nightstand in search of the lamp and switched it on. Light flooded the room, chasing away the darkness. No one else was here. Looking on the floor, thinking maybe it had been Eby brushing against my face as he'd jumped down, I failed to locate him. He was nowhere in sight.

My heart was pounding and deep within my gut I knew what I'd just experienced wasn't a dream. Still looking around the room for Eby, my gaze fell on the attic door. The chair that had been wedged beneath the knob was now turned over on its side, the door wide open, revealing the heavy, threatening darkness behind it.

CHAPTER 4

What. The. Hell. What just happened? Was it paranormal? A very vivid dream? Did I sleepwalk and open the door to the attic myself?

As a fan of horror books and movies, I was fully aware of the rule stating the guy who checked on the creepy noises coming from the basement/next room/outside alone never came back, so what I did next could be looked at in a couple of ways. Either I had a healthy curiosity about who or what kept opening the door and apparently lived in the attic, or I was a stupid moron who didn't know any better, like the guy in the horror movies. Whatever the case, it was fight or flight time and I was just curious or stupid enough to go investigate.

I inched closer to the open door, the humid, stifling heat nearly pummeling me back towards the bed. The frigid air of last night and this morning would almost be welcome. Reaching for the light switch, I noticed a quiver in my hand, but ignored it, my eyes probing the shadows at the top of the stairs. I'd felt much braver with Finn here last night, when I didn't really think the cold air and door opening on its own could really be related to anything supernatural. Now, thoughts of something upstairs didn't seem completely out of the realm of possibility.

I took a deep breath and slowly exhaled, steadying myself before beginning my trek up the narrow stairway. Why did noises always seem amplified in the middle of the night? The creaking of the stairs might as well have been a sledgehammer pounding into the walls, it seemed so loud. Part of my brain thought flight sounded pretty good right about now and tried to kick into self-preservation mode, telling me to shut the door, get a padlock, and pretend nothing ever happened. The other part made contingency plans in case I really saw something in the attic.

My chest tightened and I half expected something to come at me once I reached the top of the stairs. I felt a trickle of sweat trailing down my back, no doubt from a combination of nervousness and heat. My foot landed on the top step and I fumbled for the light switch on my right. It wasn't there.

I was panting, running both hands over the wall, grasping for the switch. It was there somewhere - it had been there last night, light switches don't just disappear, but the stupid, over-imaginative part of my brain pictured something creeping up behind me, meat cleaver in hand, ready to hack me into a thousand little pieces. I hunched over slightly, imagining the cleaver slicing through the air toward the back of my skull, when my hand finally located the light switch and snapped it on.

Whirling around to face whatever was in the attic, I found myself staring at the same stacks of boxes from the previous evening. No hulking serial killers. No meat cleavers. Exhaling loudly, I slumped against the wall. The hair on the back of my neck was soaked with sweat and I might as well have been standing in the middle of the desert, the heat was so unbearable.

Laughing both from relief and at my overreaction, I remembered that Eby hadn't been lying beside me, the attic door had been open, and his curiosity had gotten him in trouble more than once, so I needed to look around for him. Stepping forward, a loud crunch sound echoed in the room and every hair on my head stood on end. Looking down, I carefully lifted my foot and saw a packing peanut that must have fallen out of one of the moving boxes. If Finn were here, he'd be laughing his ass off at me.

I shook it off and peered around the dusty, dark-cornered attic and its numerous stacks of boxes and called out, "Eby?" My voice cracked as if I were a 13-year-old again.

No response from him, so I checked between the boxes to see if he was hiding, waiting to jump out on me. He loved playing that game. No sign of him, but other than the storage boxes, all I saw was dust and some bits of insulation. Nothing out of the ordinary. Scanning the room one more time just to double check, I decided I'd experienced a very vivid dream.

Moonlight was streaming through the window in the far left hand corner, drawing my gaze in that direction. A large box sat by itself, the lid open and filled to the brim with my old soccer balls, some smaller ones from when I'd first started playing. Smiling, I went over to look at them and maybe relive some good memories.

Squatting down to sort through the box, my elbow nudged one of the balls and it bounced across the floor a couple of times before I stopped it. When I picked it up to toss it back in the box, I noticed a splotch of red on one side. It was glistening, like the spot was wet, and after running my finger across the ball, I brought it closer for a sniff.

I knew that smell. With the multitude of soccer injuries I'd received over the years, the copperish tangy aroma of blood was all too familiar. Wait - blood? Was Eby injured somewhere up here? But I'd looked around and knew for certain he wasn't here. Had I stepped on something and cut myself? When I looked down to check my feet, that's when I saw it. A circular pool of blood on the floor about a foot in diameter. How had I missed this? It hadn't been here when Finn and I were looking around last night. One of us would have noticed it.

So how did blood get here in the past twenty-four hours?

Then I felt it. Frigid air wrapped itself around me, like it was a living, breathing entity, causing me to gasp. When I let out a shaky exhale, I could see my breath. In a 90 plus degree attic. My gaze shot down to the floor where the blood had been.

It was gone.

I lifted a trembling hand to check my finger. Clean.

Staggering backwards, I knocked over a stack of boxes, but didn't stop to pick them up. Nothing could have kept me from getting back downstairs.

. . . . .

After stumbling down the creaking stairs and nearly diving headfirst down the last several, I slammed the door shut, and wedged the chair back under the door knob. I hadn't even turned off the lights, but my hands were shaking so badly, I probably couldn't have managed it.

My chest was heaving and I lurched over to the bed, close to collapsing as the adrenaline left my body. I sat staring at the blocked attic door, just in case someone – or something – tried to come through. The chair. I'd been so relieved at not finding anything upstairs, I'd forgotten about the chair being turned over.

I'd like to think I'm a level-headed kind of guy, but what was going on? What just happened? How could it be....? What did I feel...? How did the door...?

Questions rolled around in my head, bouncing off the walls, seeking some sort of logical explanation. Maybe Eby had jumped on the chair and knocked it over, pulling the door open. It was possible, but the chair hitting the floor should have woken me. If Eby hadn't been responsible for opening the door, what had caused the chair to fall over? Then I remembered how Eby had acted this morning when he'd been playing with the Skittle in my floor and batted it under the attic door. Something had scared him and he'd high-tailed it out of here. He'd been staring at the door when he'd hissed. Like something had been behind it. And the blood?

I couldn't come up with a logical explanation. And I was possibly hallucinating.

I'd watched tons of horror movies and sat through those ghost hunter show marathons on TV and knew what the cold areas were supposed to mean. Did I believe in ghosts? I didn't disbelieve. I'd never personally *seen* a ghost, but there seemed to be some compelling evidence out there that some people had. I was open to the prospect of their existence.

Okay, I'd just say it - maybe our house was haunted. We'd only lived here a few months and with Mom being a realtor, I knew we'd gotten a good deal, but it had never occurred to me to ask why, because it wasn't high on my list of priorities. It was a place to live that didn't hold sad reminders of my Dad in every room. Didn't people sell houses for major discounts when there was something wrong with them? Like if they were haunted, built on an Indian burial ground, or inhabited by demonic spirits? Look at what happened to those people in *The Amityville Horror*, *Poltergeist*, and all the *Paranormal Activity* movies.

Was I crazy for considering this? Talking to Mom was at the top of my agenda for tomorrow. For tonight, though, I wasn't comfortable being in my room and thought maybe I'd sleep on the couch in the living room, just in case. You could never be too careful.

. . . . .

Slamming cabinet doors in the kitchen woke me the next morning. Mom wasn't known for her stealth mode when she was cooking, so Maddie and I were used to hearing pans rattling, drawers banging, and the occasional string of words Mom preferred I didn't use when something would go wrong with a recipe or she cut herself.

Blanket wrapped around me, I trudged into the kitchen and saw Mom bending over one of the cabinets, shuffling around numerous pans, the ear-splitting clanging causing Eby to whiz past me in search of cover.

"Morning, Mom. What are you doing up so early?" I asked, sliding onto a bar stool.

"Good morning, sweetie. Did I wake you? Have you seen my muffin pan?" she asked, moving on to another cabinet.

"I wouldn't know a muffin pan if it smacked me in the head. So why are you up so early?" I repeated.

"I have to drop off Maddie at her friend's house and then show a couple of houses. I'll be finished in time for your game, though."

"Um, yeah, about showing houses. Remember when we moved a few months ago and you said we'd gotten a great deal on the price of this house? Why was that?"

She'd finally found what must have been the muffin pan, because she began putting those paper cup things in it. "What, you don't think your mother's mad negotiation skills were enough to get a good price?" she teased.

"Not dissing your negotiation skills, Mom, but were there any other reasons? I remember you saying the builder was really motivated. It's a new house, so why was that?"

She stirred the batter and I thought maybe she wasn't going to answer. "You're right. There was a reason the builder was anxious to get rid of the house. It was completed in early spring, but he was anxious to get it off his inventory," she said, spooning strawberry-flavored batter into the muffin cups. Maddie's favorite

"Why? The other houses around here seem to move pretty fast."

Still working with the batter, she glanced up at me through the bangs that had fallen over her eyes. "There was another reason. Although it might have kept other buyers away, it didn't have any bearing on my decision to buy this house."

"You're killing me here, Mom, what was the reason?"

"Remember the teenage girl from your high school that went missing around the same time? Sarah Butler?"

"I didn't know her, but I remember when she disappeared. There were flyers everywhere and the police were at school searching through her locker. Didn't they find something that made them think she'd been hurt?"

After putting the pan in the oven, she turned to face me again. "Yes, they did. Some blood was found in a house under construction and it was a match with Sarah's DNA."

It felt like a brick had settled in the pit of my stomach. "You're not saying this was the house."

"That's what I'm saying."

"Why would you still buy it, knowing something must have happened here?"

"I thought about it and discussed it with some other realtor friends and decided that even if something had happened in this house, it wouldn't be a factor in our decision to buy it. This is a beautiful home, one that would have been out of our price range if the builder wasn't in such a rush to sell, and it kept you and Maddie in the same school district with your friends. After your father's accident, I knew staying in our old house wasn't an option, and I couldn't bear the thought of you going through any more disruptions. Besides, the police were never able to prove what may or may not have happened here. There were no witnesses, no one knew why Sarah had been in this house, and her body was never found. As far as I know, the case remains open and there's still the possibility she was a runaway."

Mom could think whatever she wanted, but I was almost sure Sarah wasn't a runaway and whatever happened to her may have occurred in this house. And she might not have left. "It doesn't bother you that a teenage girl might have been killed here?" I asked.

Mom came around the island and sat beside me, placing her hand over one of mine. "Cain, it would be a horrible, horrible thing if that's what happened to her. That's probably why the house didn't sell earlier, but I'm not a superstitious person. The police found no other evidence of foul play. If Sarah was a runaway, maybe she was hiding out here and accidentally hurt herself. At this point, it's all speculation.

"Whatever happened, it's in the past and if you want to get into all that stuff about residual negative energy, or whatever they call it, I don't believe in it. Even if it were true, we're a family that's struggling to move on after suffering a tremendous loss and giving off positive energy should cancel out anything negative, right?"

"I don't think it works like that," I muttered, running my other hand through my hair.

"I choose to believe maybe that poor girl was hiding out here for a period of time and is still alive out there somewhere. It's tragic for her parents, not knowing what happened to her, and I can't imagine what they must be going through."

Mom paused for a moment and looked out the window, absently

chewing her bottom lip, her shoulders heavy, and I knew she was thinking of Dad. Every now and then, I'd see her tear up, but she'd try to hide it from Maddie and me. Sometimes at night when I left Maddie's room after reading to her I'd hear Mom crying in her room. She and my Dad were married for over twenty years, but they were still gooey in love with each other and acted like teenagers at times. I thought it was embarrassing, but Finn said I should appreciate it after what happened between his parents. Although his mom had seemed to love his dad, he'd discovered she'd been having affairs for years and the divorce was bitter and ugly. Finn was right. I hadn't realized how lucky I was that my parents' marriage had been so stable.

Wherever she'd gone, she snapped back to the present. "Anyway, I'm not bothered about what may or may not have happened here and I didn't think you would be either. What's wrong, Cain? A big boy like you afraid of ghosts?" she asked, a teasing grin on her face. "I set the timer on the muffins. Can you get them out of the oven when they're ready while I shower?"

"Sure, Mom," I replied, as she left the kitchen. Now I had something else to add to my agenda for today. Finding out all I could about Sarah Butler and what had gone on in this house.

CHAPTER 5

If Sarah's ghost was really living in the attic, it seemed a little rude and all kinds of wrong to be researching her on the Internet, like she'd be looking over my shoulder or something, so I took my laptop outside on the screened porch. As embarrassing as it was to admit, I remembered when she'd disappeared, because everyone had been talking about it at school, but then I'd lost interest. Sarah hadn't been someone I'd really known - yes, it was awful something bad might have happened to her, but it wasn't anything that directly affected me, so I went on about my life. Now I was wishing I'd paid more attention.

I went to the *Post and Courier* website and found several articles, the first from February of this year, stating how Sarah's parents had reported her missing and the police were asking for any information that might help in locating her. They'd received a lot of tips, but nothing had led to her being found.

The next article talked about the possibility of Sarah being a runaway. She'd hadn't had a cell phone, a fact that was totally surreal to me in this day and age, so there were no records pulled or signals to track. She'd been somewhat of a loner at school and didn't have many friends who could offer any reasons as to why she might have run away. Her parents and teachers stated she was an excellent student, at the top of her class, there was no trouble at home, and Sarah had never been a disciplinary problem either at school or home. Her parents were convinced she'd been kidnapped, or worse.

The third article was what I'd been looking for. Four days after Sarah's disappearance, construction workers reported finding blood at one of their building sites, and it didn't belong to any of the employees. They hadn't reported it earlier because, due to other concurrent projects, it was the first time in five days they'd been back to the site. Tests confirmed the blood was a match for Sarah's DNA. The article went on to say there was no other evidence indicating if she'd been with someone or alone, and without any witnesses, it couldn't be determined if the blood was from a major or minor injury. Something had been used to wipe it up, because blood was smeared across the floor, but whatever it was hadn't been found.

A shudder ran through my body when I read the next paragraph, and my mouth dropped open. Sarah's blood had been found in a corner of the attic.

I bet I knew which corner.

. . . . . .

I spent the rest of the morning reading articles online and going through my old yearbooks. Like Mom said, the police had reached a dead end with the case and had exhausted all leads. There was no sign of Sarah and no one had come forward with any suggestions. Her parents were offering a reward for any information that could lead to her being located, dead or alive; they just wanted to know what had happened to her and find some closure.

There weren't many pictures of Sarah in the yearbook. She didn't seem to have been a very social person, only appearing in pictures of the honor society and science club. Anyway, all this needed to be put on the backburner for the time being. Finn would be here soon to pick me up and I needed to concentrate on the soccer game.

. . . . . .

As awkward, uneasy, and generally oblivious as I was with girls, when I walked onto a soccer field, things were entirely different. This was what I knew. I'd been playing soccer since the age of four and it was love at first kick. My parents had always been supportive, hauling me around with travel teams when I was too young for the school team and also during the off season. Now I was captain and center forward, on my home field, and in my comfort zone. Nothing else existed for me during a game – I was completely focused on what happened within the white outlined grass rectangle with the other seventeen players on the field.

My mind began going through strategies, plays, and what I knew about the other team and their players. Their keeper was pretty good – not as good as Finn, but I'd have to be at the top of my game to get anything past him to score.

Finn and I always arrived at the games earlier than required so we could get in some extra warmup time. We'd been playing together for so long it always seemed as if we needed this time together to get in the right mindset. It was routine for us and some athletes were so superstitious they believed any variance from their routines would curse their game. That didn't really describe us, but Finn was the best keeper in the league and, not to brag, but I'd made all-state the past three years, so warming up together challenged us, with me trying to get the ball past him and Finn contorting his body in all different manners to stop me.

While we stretched afterwards, I filled Finn in on what had happened last night in the attic and everything I'd learned from Mom and my research this morning.

"I don't know, Cain, I mean, don't you think you might be overreacting a little? So there was a cold spot in your attic. I'm no expert, but there's probably a plausible explanation. The odds of it being some bizarre air flow problem are bound to be higher than the possibility of some teenage ghost girl living in your attic and giving you scalp massages while you sleep."

"What about the blood they found in that same corner?"

"Dude, if someone leaving blood behind meant they'd return to haunt the place, don't you think the hospitals would be overrun with ghosts?"

"Finn, we live in one of the most historical cities in the country. Word is, there are more ghosts walking the streets than people."

"I love a good ghost story as much as the next guy, but remember when we hung out at the cemetery? It was a waste of time and the only thing we saw was a stray dog peeing on a gravestone – and that freaked you out. What makes you think this is any different?"

Yeah, that was me. After playing tourists and going on a ghost walk through Magnolia Cemetery, we'd gotten the bright idea to set up camp by the baby carriage tombstone, hoping to make contact with a spirit. The wispy clouds partially covering the full moon had made it a perfect night for grave watching, and we'd waited in the darkness beneath a towering oak tree draped with Spanish moss, convinced it was only a matter of time before the spirits emerged from their graves.

And the only reason the dog had scared me was because he'd sneaked up behind me and was kind of big. Maybe all I needed to do to meet a ghost was hang out in my own bedroom.

"What about the chair under the door?"

"You could have been sleeping deeper than you thought and I've seen Eby do worse than knock over a chair. That cat can be a monsoon of destruction when he gets going."

"Yeah, maybe."

"So, get rid of the ball and chain yet?"

I stretched out on the grass, hands behind my head, facing away from the sun. "I don't know what to say to her, Finn. I need to break up with her, but she's so used to getting her way, she'd probably just tell me that wasn't an option, buy me more clothes, and force me to watch another marathon of that vampire series."

"It's really not such a bad show, you know, if you can look past all those male model types. It's got some hot girls," he said, pushing his headband into place in an attempt to restrain his mop of chaotic hair. Lindsey's comparison to Harry Potter's had been pretty accurate.

"Still not worth it. No one ever dies on that show. They come back, turn into vampires, hybrids, it's hard to keep up."

"Dude, it's a little scary you know that much about it. Are you sure you're not into it?"

"Forget the vampires, alright? We need to focus on the real problem – Erin."

"Cain, you knew what she was before you went out with her. So tell her the truth. It's not you, it's her. If she screams like a banshee or comes at you with those freaky pink claws of hers, you've got to stand your ground and take it like a man."

"You're right. I know you're right," I said, rubbing my face, then running my hands through my hair.

"Suck it up, my friend. She's slowly killing your spirit. And she sure doesn't like me. What's up with that? I'm socially acceptable in most circles," Finn said, a crooked grin on his face.

"You know, you're not half as amazing as you think," I said, squinting up at him.

"What's not to love? Hey, I got a new shirt today – says 'Free Hugs' on the front and 'Champion Slut Hugger' on the back. You like?"

"I like," I said, snorting. "Get one for me – maybe that will cause Erin to break up with me instead."

"Is she coming to the game?"

"She never misses an opportunity to wear my jersey. I don't get this whole social ladder thing and how I even rank. Who decides this and who, outside of her friends, gives a crap? But if you ask her who scored or even who won the game when it's over, she won't be able to tell you. She'll probably just sit there with her friends and talk about shoes the whole time. At least I won't have to deal with her."

Enough with Erin. It was a fantastic day for a soccer game with a cloudless sky, gentle breeze, and swaying palm trees, the temperature in the mid-seventies, a miracle for Charleston, SC in September.

· · · · ·

"And then when you kicked the ball between that other guy's legs and went around him and got the ball again and scored, that was just really cool!" Maddie, Mom, Finn, and I were rehashing the highlights of the game over the pizzas Mom had picked up for dinner. I'd used the excuse of Family Night and gotten out of going to the party with Erin. Since she'd gone to all the trouble of choosing the clothes I'd wear to the party, she'd screeched her displeasure with me, but I didn't care. I was where I wanted to be. "And then when you kicked the ball a really long way and it went right over the guy's head and into the net and scored again, that was even better!"

"Sounds like someone's got a little bit of hero worship," Mom muttered so Maddie couldn't hear.

Finn reached over and yanked lightly on Maddie's ponytail. "What about me, baby girl? I stopped a few balls today."

Maddie rolled her eyes. "Well, most of the time you just stand in the net and yell at the other players and tell them what to do. You're not like Cain. He gets to score the goals and win the game for the team."

"Yeah, Finn's pretty useless most of the time, but just because he doesn't score goals doesn't mean he's not helping the team, Maddie. If he didn't keep the other team from scoring, we might not win the game."

Maddie put her arms on the table and rested her chin in her hands, as if she were pondering that. "I guess that's true, but you always seem to know exactly where to run and what to do and how to do it to score."

Finn smirked. "Too bad you can't do that off the field, Cain. From the mouths of babes and all that."

Finn had me there. If handling my love life was as easy as playing soccer, I wouldn't be stuck in this mess.

CHAPTER 6

Sunday was all mine. I'd been waiting for this day for weeks. The Terrace Theater was showing a horror movie marathon, including some of the old classics like *The Texas Chainsaw Massacre*, *Night of the Living Dead*, and some of the better newer movies, *Sinister*, *Insidious*, and the first *Paranormal Activity*. I'd asked Finn if he was interested, and he's also a fan of horror movies, but keeping him confined for that amount of time went against the laws of nature. I'd never planned on asking Erin. For one thing, I'd never be able to enjoy myself and for another, she considered horror movies a waste of time. As opposed to shopping for more clothes today to add to her overflowing closet. Which wasn't a waste of time at all. So I was on my own. Happily.

After stopping at concessions for a large buttered popcorn, a root beer, and chocolate chip cookie dough, I went to one of the smaller theaters to find the perfect seat. Not so close that I had to crane my neck, but not all the way in the last row either. The sweet spot was halfway back, middle of the row. I'd just gotten settled and dug my hand into the greasy goodness of the buttery popcorn, when someone leaned over the back of the seat beside me.

"So which movie are you most excited to see on the big screen? *Texas Chainsaw* or *Night of the Living Dead*?" she asked, her sandy blonde hair falling over the chair and brushing my arm. Her citrusy cinnamon smell was familiar and comforting, almost like coming home.

"Lindsey?" I asked, twisting in my seat so I could see her. "What are you doing here?"

"You mean this isn't the chick-flick damsel in distress movie marathon?" she asked, her mouth falling open, feigning shock. "Same reason you're here, I'm guessing. A love of horror movies. Can I sit with you or would it interfere with your viewing experience?"

Was this a trick question? "No."

"No I can't sit with you?"

"Yes. No! No, you won't interfere with the movies and yes, you can definitely sit with me."

"Ling and Emma were supposed to come with me, but when I invited them, I might have left out the part about this being a horror marathon. Anyway, when they found out, they decided to ditch me and go to that new indoor rock climbing place. Wimps. Anyway, here I am alone, with no date."

A wide grin split my face as she climbed over the back of the chair and sat beside me. Whatever I did to deserve this was a mystery, but I planned to totally enjoy it. Could this day get any better?

. . . . .

Seeing the older movies on the big screen was a real treat, but experiencing this with the horror fangirl beside me was even better. Besides being knowledgeable about the flicks themselves, Lindsey also knew her movie etiquette and didn't interrupt or ask questions during the showings, something I really appreciated.

After the last movie, we walked a few doors down to Zia Taqueria. Since the music was a little too loud inside, we got a table outside in the balmy, slightly breezy evening.

"I can't believe I never knew you liked horror movies."

"It never came up, I guess," Lindsey said, scooping a healthy amount of salsa onto her tortilla chip.

We sat in silence for a few minutes, but it wasn't uncomfortable. Erin had always felt the need to fill every minute with mindless babbling, most of which I tuned out.

Lindsey's hand inched across the table to cover mine. "I didn't know you when we first moved here last year, and I've wanted to say this for a while, but I know what happened with your dad, and I'm really sorry. I can't imagine going through anything like that."

Her hand was so warm and small compared to mine, but strong, probably from playing the cello. Taking a deep breath and hoping my palms weren't too sweaty, I turned my hand over to hold hers. And she didn't pull away.

"Thanks. It was hard and still is some of the time. I mean, I still miss him every day and I don't think my Mom will ever completely get over his death, but I feel sorrier for my sister Maddie. I had seventeen years with him, but she only got seven and I wonder if she'll still remember him in ten years."

"You and your Mom will help her remember if she forgets. There are probably pictures and videos too, right?"

I smiled, remembering how my parents had always been big on taking pictures and recording both important and everyday family moments. Our house was covered with pictures and although it had hurt at first seeing Dad in so many frames, happy and enjoying his family, now they brought back warm, good memories. "Yeah, we've got a lot to show her. I try to do some of the things with her that he always did, like reading to her before bedtime and building Legos. She's kind of clumsy and doesn't have any interest in sports or girly things, like dolls, but she's got an incredible imagination and builds things I'd never think of."

Lindsey squeezed my hand. "It sounds like you really love her. I think that's sweet."

I ducked my head and stared at her through a strand of hair that had fallen out of my leather tie. "Yeah, she's pretty cool. But I feel like I'm all they've got now, and I need to take on what I can of my Dad's responsibilities. With Mom being a realtor, she's got some crazy hours sometimes, and Finn helps out when he can."

"Cain, I've never met your Mom, but from what you've told me about her, I'm sure she doesn't expect you to take your Dad's place and, although I'm sure she appreciates you helping with Maddie, she would want you to live your life and be a teenager."

"Are you sure you've never met her?" I asked, tucking the strand of hair behind my ear with the hand that wasn't holding hers. "That's almost exactly what she told me a couple of nights ago."

Lindsey looked down at our hands and opened her mouth to say something, but the waiter arrived with our shrimp tacos. Whatever she'd been about to say, the moment had passed and since we both needed to eat, I reluctantly let go of her. At that moment, I wished more than anything that I was free to hold her hand whenever I wanted, but knew as long as Erin was technically still my 'girlfriend', it wasn't a possibility. But it sure was an incentive.

. . . . .

When I got home that evening, I read the next chapter of *The Prisoner of Azkaban* to Maddie. We'd just gotten to the part where Harry discovered Sirius was his godfather, and Maddie gasped out loud.

Once I kissed her goodnight and Mom tucked her in, I stopped in the kitchen to feed Eby, made sure all the doors were locked and lights were off, then went to my bedroom to finish the next chapter of *Gone With the Wind*. I'd much rather be reading *Harry Potter*.

As soon as I flicked on the light, I froze and felt the hairs on the back of my neck prickle. Strange things had been going on in my room today during my absence.

The attic door was open again, which was pretty routine lately, but my posters had been ripped from the walls and were lying on the floor, along with some PS4 discs that had been torn from their plastic cases. Thankfully, they were all still intact. The posters were inexpensive, but I had hundreds of dollars invested in the games.

If I'd had a brat sister with no sense of boundaries, that's who I'd look to first, but I knew Maddie hadn't done this. She had several PS4 Lego games, Jurassic World her current favorite, and they were also scattered around the room.

I wasn't a psychologist, but even I understood these were the actions of someone seeking attention. What had it been like when Sarah was trashing my room – even more than it already was? Did it look like an invisible force had been unleashed and was bent on destruction? Or was she more of an opaque entity? Then my gut twisted and I slumped against the doorway. What if Maddie had come in here to play video games or Mom had been putting away laundry during all the havoc? Would they have been just an obstacle in Sarah's path? Would she have hurt them? Was that even a possibility?

Forget Finn's logical explanation rationale. I needed to come up with a way to make contact with Sarah, or whoever was trying to communicate with me.

While putting the posters and games back where they belonged, I remembered the comment Lindsey had made earlier about pictures and videos and an idea began to form. I jogged downstairs to the coat closet in the foyer and fumbled through extra blankets, gloves, and umbrellas before finding what I'd been looking for. Dad's old camcorder. Before he began using his phone to record, Dad's camcorder had been like an extra appendage at soccer games or family outings and he'd taught me how to operate it. Which was exactly what I planned to do.

CHAPTER 7

The next morning, I was awakened by Mom gently shaking my shoulder. "Cain, sweetie, you overslept and you're going to be late for school. You need to get up. Didn't you set your alarm?"

"Mom? What time is it?"

"It's ten minutes before you normally leave. I would have gotten you up earlier if I'd known you'd overslept, but Maddie was having a wardrobe malfunction and I was dealing with that in her bedroom. You get dressed and I'll fix a quick breakfast you can take with you."

Crap. After setting up the camcorder last night, I'd forgotten to turn on my alarm and now I'd have to wait until this evening after soccer practice to watch the recording. Luckily, I'd showered last night, so I threw on some relatively clean jeans lying on the floor, grabbed the first t-shirt I saw, and pulled my hair back.

Stumbling through the debris on my floor, I went over to the dresser to turn off the camcorder. It was gone. This was where I'd set it up last night, so what could have happened to it? I looked on the floor in front of the dresser and behind it thinking Eby, with his infinite supply of curiosity and grace, might have knocked if off, but it wasn't in either of those places. I turned around, my eyes combing the room, searching for the camcorder among the discarded food bags, empty Gatorade bottles, and dirty clothes.

Then I froze as my gaze fell upon it, lying on its side in front of my closet door. Which was on the other side of the room. Eby definitely hadn't done that.

· · · · ·

"You're saying you recorded yourself sleeping?" Finn and I were walking through the student parking lot to the field house after school to change clothes before soccer practice. "Don't you think that's a little kinky? Do you do things in your sleep I should know about? Wait – don't answer that. I probably don't want to know."

"I positioned the recorder on my dresser so my bed and the attic door were both in the frame, but then this morning, it was lying on the floor across the room. After the mess I came home to last night, I'm hoping we'll see something when I play it back."

Finn opened the locker room door, releasing the revolting odors of practice clothes long past their expiration date, musty lockers and showers, and stiff towels in desperate need of washing. It was surprising that after so many years of spending time in there, my sniffer still functioned at all.

Finn looked at me, disbelief written all over his face. "Wait, you're saying it was lying across the room this morning. And you don't know how it got there."

"Yep," I said, popping the p.

"Alright, you're my excuse. I'm supposed to be with my other parental figure tonight, although it's even a stretch to call her that, but I've been looking for a reason not to go. Did I tell you she's living with a new guy? The guy from last month, Glen, moved out."

"I thought his name was Joel."

"He was the guy from last spring. It's hard to keep them straight. Sometimes I'm not sure she even knows their names, there've been so many. Anyway, not that I'm looking forward to observing your nocturnal habits, but I hope we can solve the mystery of your attic door and how the camcorder came to be across the room with a logical explanation."

"Well, good luck with that," I said, slamming my locker door closed.

• • • • •

"Bro, your mom's shrimp and grits are legendary. You have to let me know when she makes this. I'm serious. Every. Time."

We'd been anxious to watch the recording, but our empty stomachs cried out for sustenance, so dinner came first. Mom was so used to Finn showing up, she always made extra then gave him leftovers to take home to his dad. Unless Finn kept them for himself.

Finn connected the camcorder to the television in my bedroom and, considering I hadn't gone to bed until 1 am and then was awakened by Mom

42

at 7 am, we only had six hours to rewind. As we watched from the gamer chairs, the first hour showed me tossing and turning before finally settling down, and then Eby showed up soon after, jumping onto the bed, sniffing my head, then curling up at my side.

Other than me shifting in sleep, nothing out of the ordinary happened until around 3 am. Eby's head shot up, his gaze focused on the attic door, then he slowly stood, back arching, tail bushy and tall. He let out an eerie yowl I'm surprised didn't have me shooting out of the bed in a panic, then leaped off the bed and out of the frame.

As we watched the attic door open inch by inch, I didn't know if I'd be able to hear any audio over the blood pounding through my veins and wiped my sweaty palms on the sides of the chair. In hopes of making visualization a little easier during playback, I'd left a light on in the bathroom while I'd slept, but the details were still a little murky.

Despite what Finn had said about malfunctioning air ducts and pressure from within the house, in the back of my mind I'd always known that wasn't the cause. Maybe it was wishful thinking on my part, hoping to make contact with something otherworldly, but seeing it on screen while I lay helpless and unaware in my bed had me rethinking that hope.

The attic door stopped abruptly when it was nearly completely open, and we saw no other movement. At first.

On the screen, I was lying on my back, one arm thrown overhead, the other hand resting on my bare chest, my face partially obscured by a few strands of hair. Then, my hair gently moved away from my face, although I hadn't moved, not even a subtle shift of my body.

Okay. That happened.

"Alright, that isn't proof of anything. You've got wavy hair and maybe the weight of it just shifted from when Eby jumped off the bed."

"Shut up and watch." I was anxious and wanted to make sure we didn't miss seeing or hearing anything.

Barely a minute passed before the hand resting on my chest rose until my arm was extended diagonally, then moved subtly back and forth. It looked almost like....but it was impossible. Wasn't it? Tremors shot down my spine. Seeing myself doing this on the screen was surreal, like I was watching someone else.

"Dude, it looks like you're stroking someone's face," Finn said, which was exactly what I'd been thinking. "What are you doing?"

"I'm wondering the same thing."

Suddenly, my arm dropped heavily back to my chest, the covers shifted on the edge of the bed beside me, and a t-shirt lying at the foot of the bed shot up into the air, then flew across the room, striking the front of my desk and falling to the floor. No more than a couple of seconds later, the camcorder jumped a few inches to the right, causing both Finn and me to let out startled yelps.

Something seemed to pass in front of the camcorder and for a moment, the screen was milky white, then everything became blurry and indistinguishable. There was a loud crack as the camcorder hit the closet door and fell to the floor, where I'd found it this morning. The screen went to static, then black.

CHAPTER 8

When the recording went black, other than the hiss of the air conditioner, the room was silent as Finn and I continued to gape in shock at the television screen. He spoke first.

"Cain, how did the camcorder get on the other side of the room?"

I snorted. "Finn, if I knew the answer to that, would I have asked for your help?"

More silence. "What caused your t-shirt to fly through the air and moved the blanket on your bed?"

Sighing heavily, I said, "I need answers, not more questions. You think I'm not wondering the same thing?"

"Alright, I have an idea. Where the screen went filmy white, I want to rewind to that part and freeze it to see if we can make out anything."

While Finn forwarded and rewound several times, trying to find the right frame, I stared at the attic door. All had been quiet this evening after the chaos of last night. What we had on the recording was proof something was in the attic – and in my room. Shuddering involuntarily, I thought about whatever it was touching me while I slept. And I must have been sleeping like the dead last night not to have woken up. Okay, maybe not the best word choice.

Finn swore, bringing my attention back to him. "Um, Cain? I have something, and you're probably not going to like this."

Turning my head, I studied the screen, my mouth dropping open. I really shouldn't have been so surprised. Staring back at me, her face contorted in anger, was the semi-transparent figure of Sarah Butler.

"Okay."

"Woah."

"Yeah."

"This is real, and she's living in my attic."

"What should we do now?"

"Finn, you're just full of obvious questions tonight, aren't you? Could you maybe use that brain power to come up with some answers?"

"Hey, whose idea was it to freeze frame Sarah? Oh, that's right, it was me. It's your turn to come up with an idea."

Subconsciously, I'd known what would happen if we managed to prove Sarah, or something else, was here, but I'd pushed it to the back of my mind because I wasn't sure how to go about it. And wasn't really sure if I wanted to. "We have to figure out how to communicate with her."

Finn leaned back and crossed his arms over his chest. "Cain, Sarah didn't look like Casper the Friendly Ghost in that frame, you know what I'm saying? Are you sure you want to try and contact her? Maybe we should just get a priest or something."

"She hasn't tried to hurt me or anyone else. Maybe she just didn't want to be recorded, I don't know. We've been here all these months and things are just now starting to happen, so there must be a reason for it. What if she wants us to get a message to her parents or let us know what happened to her?"

Finn uncrossed his arms, his shoulders dropping slightly. "Yeah, that could be a possibility. Okay, should we invite her downstairs for tea and scones? Play some video games? Get a Ouija board? I'm a little unclear about the etiquette here."

"I guess we could, um…well…..I'm a little unclear myself, and I've never used a Ouija board. Maybe we could Google it? Doesn't Google have answers for everything?"

"Sure it does. We've got to start somewhere. So, we'll both do some research tonight, see what we've come up with in the morning and make a plan. I'll grab those leftovers in the fridge and head on home, unless you need me to stay. You got this covered or do you need a wing man?"

"Nah, I'm good. We'll talk in the morning."

I didn't need Finn to stay over, but there was no way I was staying in my room tonight, not after what I'd seen on the recording. Thinking about Sarah being in my bedroom while I slept, touching my hair and sitting on my bed, seemed a little stalkerish and just plain freaky to me, so after Finn left, I did my nightly reading with Maddie, then made myself comfortable on the living room couch for the rest of the night.

. . . . .

The next morning offered a better start to my day. I'd remembered to set my alarm and was out of the living room before Mom could ask any questions resulting in some pretty awkward answers. From our earlier conversation, I knew she didn't believe in ghosts and wasn't superstitious and the last thing she needed was something else to worry about, so I was determined to handle this on my own.

When I went upstairs to shower, my room looked undisturbed from the previous night. I'd been thinking about how to communicate with Sarah and had decided to try a direct approach, which is probably something I should commit to in other parts of my life.

I cleared my throat and wiped my hands on my pajama pants. "Um…Sarah? Are you here? Can we talk?" Admittedly, I felt a little ridiculous standing in the middle of my bedroom talking to a ghost who may or may not be able to answer me. But I guessed it was no different than talking to Eby. Except, of course, that Eby answered me, and we'd had some very enlightening conversations. After a couple of minutes with no response, no doors opening or pockets of cold air, I gave up and went into the bathroom to shower.

Maybe I'd stayed in the shower longer than I thought, because when I pulled back the curtain, it looked like a fog bank had rolled in. After wrapping a towel around my waist, I raised my hand to wipe off the mirror and froze, the blood in my veins turning to ice. Written in the condensation on the mirror were four words.

'I'm here. Help me.'

. . . . .

It took several beats of my heart – at least, I think my heart was still beating – before I could move my arms and legs again. Ho-ly crap. Could things get any more bizarre around here? Okay, Cain, stop tempting fate. You're just begging for a bigger creep show than you've already got.

I lifted my hand to the mirror, but the condensation trickling down the silvery surface was distorting the message. Opening the bathroom door a couple of inches, I peeked into my room on the off chance someone was messing with me, playing a trick. As expected, no one else was here.

But the attic door was standing wide open - something that didn't shock me at all.

During lunch, I gave Finn a brief account of what had happened this morning before the Wicked Witch of the West got here. Communicating with Sarah tonight had to be put on the back burner, because of the soccer game this evening.

"Incoming on your left. She decided to ride her broom today instead of carrying the pitchfork," Finn said, nearly causing me to snort milk through my nose. Wouldn't have been the first time.

I glanced sideways and saw that Erin was wearing ridiculously high heels that couldn't have been comfortable, and an expression that gave her a constantly surprised look. Finn said it had something to do with over-plucked eyebrows. How he'd know that, I didn't care to ask.

She sat beside me, but kept looking over her shoulder at the table where her posse were watching. "Cain, did you bring your jersey for me to wear tonight?"

"Good afternoon to you too, Erin, and how was your weekend?" Finn asked, his face the picture of innocence.

"Finn, you know I never answer your questions and what I did over the weekend is *so* not any of your business."

"Well, Cain and I would prefer not to see your face at our lunch table every day either, but I don't recall you giving us a choice."

Erin turned to me, her lips pressed in a hard line. "Is that true, Cain? Don't you want me to sit with you at lunch?"

"Well, um…" I looked to Finn for help, but he held both hands out, looking very pleased with himself, like he'd just served me Erin's head on a silver platter.

"Cain?" Keeping in mind my inability to read women, I decided to err on the side of caution and attempt to calm the wild expression in Erin's eyes that made me think she bordered on creating a very public scene.

"I never said that, Erin. Finn's just playing around." Finn sighed loudly, probably planning to look for a new best friend who wasn't such a coward.

"And what about your jersey?" she spat.

"I'll bring it to the game tonight." Flipping her hair over her shoulder and giving Finn a triumphant smirk, Erin picked up her tray and marched across the cafeteria toward her friends, high heels clacking in her wake.

"Next time, rethink the eyebrow wax, sweetheart," Finn called as she strutted away, turning to make an obscene gesture at him before she sat down. "Dude, I gave you the perfect opening, and you threw it away. If you want to wallow in misery, that's your stupid choice. But Lindsey won't wait forever."

. . . . .

The competition was brutal. We were playing smart and hard, but by the end of the first half, the score was tied at 1-1. Five shots on goal, and we'd only scored once, when I'd headed the ball into the upper left hand corner. Finn had made three saves, his body twisting in positions that looked physically impossible.

After a motivational speech and some new strategic moves from Coach Simms at half-time, the team was locked and loaded, ready to get back on the field. We fought hard, dribbling and swerving around opponents, blocking kicks, passing and stealing the ball, but when it came down to the last two minutes, the score was still tied. And then we got lucky when their right mid fielder fouled me, receiving a yellow card and giving me a penalty kick.

Taking a deep breath, I studied the other team's keeper as he crouched in preparation, readying himself for my kick. I could do this. Charging forward, I feigned a rightward direction and the keeper bought it, lunging to that side a half second before my foot connected with the ball, but it sailed directly over him, hitting the back of the net.

The crowd roared and my teammates ran over to congratulate me, but we couldn't celebrate yet - we still had over a minute left. The center forward on the other team dribbled down the field and got past our mid fielders, passing to another player close enough to take a shot on goal, but Finn easily caught the ball, found me on the field, and kicked it in my direction, placing it a couple of feet in front of me. As I got it under control, I turned and dribbled down the field toward the goal, the opposing team's defenders lined up in front of me.

The crowd was screaming, the excitement high, and I knew there wasn't much time left. I could hear Finn behind me in the keeper's box, shouting out the position of the opponents around me. As I brought my leg back and prepared to take a shot, I heard Finn's voice, the tone different, more panicked and insistent, yelling, "On your left, Shannon! Left!"

And then everything went black.

CHAPTER 9

What was that irritating sound? Like the constant buzzing of a weedeater. It just kept going on and on and wouldn't shut up, like when Erin talked about shoes, just nonstop noise grating on my nerves. Was that the cause of this pounding, throbbing headache that pulsed with every beat of my heart? I'd swear my brain was bouncing around in my skull. Even my eyes hurt, like they were too big for my head. What had happened to me?

The last thing I remembered was Finn yelling at me to watch my left side. Did I get hit? I'd been injured playing soccer before – you can't play as many years as I had without getting hurt. My left hand had a permanent impression of soccer cleats from a game five years ago when an opponent had stepped on me and was in no hurry to move on.

But this – I'd never felt pain like this in my life. Along with the headache, the left side of my body felt like I'd been hit by a semi-truck and dragged for a few miles.

And what was that weird smell? Not the smell of freshly cut grass or sweaty soccer players – but a clean smell, like an antiseptic. Where was the murmuring of the crowd and the thump of cleated feet trampling the grass? And since when did the soccer field get so soft?

But that constant drone was still going on, like a jackhammer battering my skull.

"Stop. Someone make it stop, please," I heard a voice say. It's like they could read my mind.

"Cain? Did you say something?" Mom's voice being that close pretty much confirmed I wasn't on the soccer field any longer.

"Cain, baby, I was so worried!" Erin. I should have known it was her voice making the monotonous sound of the weedeater. How had I never noticed that shrill pitch before?

"Cain, are you awake, sweetie?" Mom asked, now with the embarrassing term of endearment.

I was afraid if I opened my eyes, they'd roll out of my head, but figured that couldn't hurt any worse than the pain I already felt, so I decided to give it a shot.

Slowly, I attempted to open one eyelid – and immediately closed it again. The light coming through the blinds was like a knife stabbing my eyeball.

"For the love of all that's holy, someone close the blinds before my brain explodes." I don't know who took pity on me, but I sensed the room get a little darker and then opened one eye in a narrow slit.

"Oh, Cain, I'm so glad you're alright!" Erin said, throwing her body across my chest, wrapping her arms around my neck and jostling my head. Which made me feel like vomiting. On her.

"Would someone get her off me? Get her out of here, please!"

"Cain? I can't believe you're talking to me like that! I've been here for two hours waiting for you to wake up and you're treating me like I'm some annoying clingy girlfriend. I could have gone out with Hillary and Lauren instead of waiting here for you, but…."

"Please, just shoot me now, put me out of my misery, I'm begging you." At least I wouldn't have to listen to her incessant whining wherever I'd wind up.

"Erin, dear, maybe you should leave and let Cain get some rest. You can call tomorrow and check on him," Mom said, using the tone Maddie and I knew meant 'Do as I say, no arguing, no negotiating.'

"Fine. I've got plenty of other things to do anyway," Erin replied, spinning on her heel and marching out of the room without saying goodbye.

Thank God.

Silence, blessed silence. Cracking open the other eye, the needles of pain I'd felt from the late evening sunlight streaming through the blinds was lessened somewhat with them shut. Still painful, but bearable.

"Without touching me or moving me in any way and with quiet voices, can someone please tell me where I am and what happened?"

"What do you remember?" Mom asked.

My brain felt like mush, thoughts and memories swirling, flitting here and there as I struggled to grasp something. "I remember Finn yelling at me about someone on my left, then everything went black. But…" Despite my attempts to remember the moments right before I'd heard Finn, I drew a blank. "I can't remember anything else about the game, the score, who we were playing. What's wrong with me?"

"You're alright, Cain. The doctor said there could be some temporary memory loss. What's the last thing you remember before you heard Finn?" Mom asked.

Searching my memories, it seemed as if there were gaps – like something should be in that spot, but remained hidden. Then I had a memory that brought a smile to my face. "The movie? I had dinner with Lindsey after that, but before that some things are kind of fuzzy."

Mom's gaze flickered to a space on my left.

"Dude, that was two days ago."

Finn was here? I tried to turn toward his voice, but the ice picks stabbing my head didn't allow for that.

"Hold up, Cain, I'll move around the bed. Don't need to damage that brain more than it already is," Finn said, coming into my line of sight.

"Two days ago? What happened to me?"

"You're in the hospital, sweetie. You were injured in the soccer game," Mom replied, her hand patting my shin.

"Why can't I remember?"

"You're concussed, bro. You probably shouldn't try to think very hard, it might use up any remaining brain cells."

"You're such an ass, Finn," I said, really wanting to do him bodily harm right now.

"Hey, we've all got parts to play, just doing mine."

"You were hit on your blind side by a boy from the other team and when you fell, your head struck the ground pretty hard. You were unconscious when they brought you off the field and only woke up after the CT, although you probably don't remember that. The doctor said you may experience some short term memory loss and not to panic if everything doesn't come back to you right away. You really scared me, Cain," she said, her eyes tearing up.

"Sorry, Mom," I said, reaching for her hand and squeezing it. This must have been terrifying for her. Seeing me injured and being back here at the hospital had to have brought back painful memories of Dad.

"I was scared too, Cain. I was afraid you wouldn't wake up and would leave us like Daddy did," Maddie said, peeking out from behind Mom with red-rimmed eyes, her chin quivering. Seeing that look on her face chiseled away a piece of my heart. She'd been so quiet, I hadn't even known she was in the room. And Maddie was never that quiet.

Mom brushed her hand over Maddie's head. "I know she's too young to be in here and is technically breaking the rules, but I found a sympathetic nurse who also has young children."

"I'm sorry I scared you, Maddie," I replied, letting go of Mom's hand to stroke Maddie's cheek. "I promise I'm not going anywhere and I'll be home tomorrow. We'll read extra to make up for missing tonight, okay?" She nodded, a lop-sided grin lighting up her face as she sniffled and wiped away her tears.

"Come here, baby girl," Finn said, picking up Maddie, her arms wrapping around his neck as her head dropped to his shoulder. It had to be close to her bedtime. "It was Morgan, the centerback. I don't know what his problem was, but he must have thought he was on a football field, the way he tackled you. You were getting ready to take a shot on goal and I yelled at you to watch your left, but you didn't hear me. The ref red carded his as..," glancing at Maddie in his arms, Finn stopped himself from saying the word I knew he was really thinking. "Um, red carded him and threw him out of the game."

"Was that before or after your yellow card, Finn?" Mom asked.

I groaned. "What did you do this time?"

"It was like there was a contract on you, Cain. I've never seen anyone get hit that hard in a soccer game. Then when I saw you go down, you weren't moving and I thought...," Finn looked away, unable to continue. He rarely showed this much emotion.

Mom reached across me and patted one of Finn's hands that was supporting Maddie. "He went after the guy and it took three of your teammates to hold him back. He beat me to your side, even though I jumped the fence, and probably would have hurt the boy myself if Finn hadn't gotten there first."

I stared at Mom, knowing my face was a picture of horror and embarrassment. "You went on the field?"

"Totally justified," Finn said, able to speak again. "It was bad, Cain. They strapped you to the board and took you away in the ambulance with your Mom. I took Maddie and followed in my car and missed the rest of the game. Don't know if we won or lost." He'd been swaying side to side with Maddie, who was now sound asleep on his shoulder, a trail of drool on the sleeve of his jersey.

I felt horrible for what I'd put them through. No wonder my head felt like it was three times normal size if I'd taken a hit that hard. "I'm sorry you were so worried."

"We're just relieved you're alright, sweetie. Your CT was clear, other than the concussion, but they want to keep you here overnight for observation. Do you want me to stay with you?"

"No, I'm good, you and Maddie go home. I'll probably just sleep some more."

"Are you sure?" she asked, her forehead creased with worry.

"I'm positive. Go home and rest."

Mom had always been able to tell when I was lying, like she could probe my inner thoughts, and she was doing it now. "If you're sure, but call me if you need anything, alright?" she said, gently kissing the top of my forehead. "I'll be back to pick you up tomorrow morning."

Finn transferred Maddie from his arms to Mom's, and she glanced back at me once more as she went out the door. Finn lingered a while longer. "Just say the word, bro, and I'll kill the guy who did this to you. You didn't even have a chance to defend yourself."

"I appreciate the gesture, but dial it back, because you'd never last a day in jail. Seriously, though, thanks for sticking around and, uh, everything." Eloquent, I wasn't.

"I got your back, you got mine, right? So, dinner with Lindsey after the movie marathon. You don't remember anything after that?"

"Why? Did I forget something important? I'm guessing I'm still with Erin since she was here. That screeching voice will probably replay in my nightmares tonight."

Finn had a funny look on his face, an expression I'd never seen before. "Nothing we need to talk about right now. I gotta say, though, the way you talked to Erin when you woke up gave me hope. Try to remember how good that felt when you're off the meds. An Erin-free existence. I know it's a personal dream of mine."

No denying it – I felt lighter when she wasn't around. Or maybe it was the meds. But my body felt heavy and ached and I wanted sleep more than anything right now. "Not that I'm kicking you out, but I'm fading fast."

"Get some rest and I'll be over tomorrow after school." Finn might have said more, but I was already gone.

CHAPTER 10

Having a concussion had its perks. Mom catered to my every whim, something I could get used to. Erin hadn't called – also a perk. She was probably waiting for me to apologize – not happening. The downside was that I still had no recollection of anything after dinner with Lindsey on Sunday, and the few days prior to that were filled with some gray areas. Maybe going back to school tomorrow would jog my memory.

"Cain, you have a visitor," Mom said, poking her head through my bedroom door.

"Tell her I'm in a coma, incoherent, abducted by aliens – I really don't care, just please, don't let Erin in here."

"Um, it's not Erin," she chuckled, "although she is a girl. A very pretty one. She said her name was Lindsey."

My doofus expression must have told Mom everything.

"I see. That certainly explains things. I'll send her up," she said, a knowing look on her face.

Lindsey came to see me, so she must care a little, right? Wait, Lindsey was here to see me and I hadn't showered, combed my hair, or brushed my teeth since, when? Yesterday morning, I thought. Springing out of bed, I dodged the minefield of debris on my floor to get to the bathroom. Where I leaned against the sink to get my balance. Shouldn't have moved that fast with a bruised brain. When the room stopped spinning, I attended to what personal hygiene I could in hopes of not sending her running out the door in horror. The goal was to get her closer to me, not further away.

I'd just gotten back in bed when I heard a light knock at my door.

"Cain? Can I come in?"

"Yeah, come on in, Lindsey."

Opening the door slowly, she peeked around the corner at me, seeming a little hesitant about coming in. Seeing her was like the sun breaking through the clouds and I couldn't help the smile that spread across my face.

"Come on in and sit down."

"Um, where should I sit?"

Good question. My desk chair was covered up with dirty or clean clothes, I forgot which, and the gamer chairs were across the room in front of the TV. That left my bed.

"Oh, sorry," I said, shoving stuff onto the floor. Eby had been in a semi-comatose state on my bed and raised his head, looking highly annoyed at the disturbance.

"Wow, that's a really big cat."

"He's not fat, just a little over-fluffy. Sorry about the mess. I think there's room for you now," I said, after clearing a space at the foot of my bed.

Lindsey sat down and Eby, being the nosy cat he was, sauntered over and sat directly in front of her, his gaze intent on her face.

"Okay, that's kind of freaky. What's he doing?"

"Yeah, he's a little quirky, but a great judge of people. He's deciding if you meet his standards. Do you like cats?"

"Um, on a case by case basis, I guess. My social acceptability has never been decided by a cat. Does he ever blink?"

Eby must have deemed Lindsey acceptable, because he crawled into her lap and rubbed his head under her chin, his purring echoing through the room. He had a loud motor.

Grinning, I said, "You must be good people since Eby gave his approval."

"Thanks, I guess?" she said, petting him as he curled up against her leg. "With the question of my character out of the way, I just wanted to see how you were. That was a scary hit you took yesterday. Finn texted to let me know you were alright, but I wanted to see for myself. I hope it's okay that I came over without calling."

"Yeah, I'm glad you did." Cue the goofy smile again. If my lack of personal hygiene didn't drive her away, my inner dork would.

"Do you know the guy that hit you? It seemed so personal, like he was out to get you. And Finn was a pit bull after you hit the ground. The guy was lucky Finn wasn't able to get to him."

"I've played against that other guy for the past three years, but I don't know him. Finn's a good friend. He's always had my back."

"Does your head hurt?" Lindsey asked, still petting Eby, who was now lying spread-eagle on his back, a sucker for the attention.

"I still have a slight headache, but the worst thing is the amnesia. I don't remember anything after having dinner with you Sunday evening, and some things from a few days before that are fuzzy."

"But you remember what happened at dinner, right?" she asked, teasing me.

"Yeah, I remember," I said, glancing down and pulling at the threads on my comforter. Then I felt the warmth of her hand over mine, and I flipped my hand over to entwine our fingers.

"That's good to know. You know, Cain, if you wanted to get out of coming to my concert this week, you could have said something. I mean, don't you think this was a little over the top?"

"I guess I'm not a half-assed kind of guy," I smirked. "Seriously, I plan on coming to see you play. Just let me know the time."

"Will you be bringing a date?" she asked, peering at me through a fringe of blonde hair that had fallen over her forehead.

"Absolutely not."

"Good," she replied. "That's really good."

As Lindsey played with Eby and talked about our assignment for English, I noticed the attic door behind her slowly inch open about a foot, creaking as it moved. Eby froze, then flipped over to a crouch and stared at the door as it continued to swing open a few more inches.

Lindsey turned to see where the noise came from. "Well, that's weird. Where does that door lead?"

Before I could answer, Eby went into defense mode, his fur bristling and a low growl emanating from his throat. After a scathing hiss, he leaped from the bed and shot through the bedroom door.

"Okay, that was even weirder. Is there a cat torture chamber in there I'm not aware of?"

"No," I chuckled. "I don't know what his problem is. I guess the door wasn't latched all the way. That just leads to the attic storage."

I moved to swing my legs over the side of the bed to close the door, but Lindsey stopped me. "No, I've got it. Stay in bed."

"Sorry about the stuff in the floor," I said, as she maneuvered through the obstacle course.

"Don't worry about it. My room isn't quite this bad, but it's not perfect, either."

After closing the attic door, Lindsey shivered slightly, rubbing her arms.

"It's freezing over here. Is there an AC vent around?"

"I don't think so," I replied, my brow furrowing. Something seemed…familiar, although I couldn't figure out what.

"Is something wrong? Are you in pain?"

"No, I was just trying to remember something and I can almost… It's nothing."

"I need to get back home and work on that paper anyway. I'm really glad you weren't seriously injured, Cain. Let me know if there's something I can do to help with your memory. That would drive me crazy, missing time like that," she said, walking back to my bedside.

"Yeah, it's not a good feeling. I guess I'll see you at school tomorrow. Thanks for coming over, Lindsey."

"I'll get back to you about the concert time this week. Maybe we can do something after that. Bye, Cain," she said, leaning down and kissing me on the cheek. When she got to the bedroom door, she turned once more and waved, leaving me speechless.

That. Just. Happened. Lindsey kissed me. Sure, it was on the cheek, but it was still a kiss and it counted. Did she ask me out? First thing on the agenda for tomorrow, find a way to break up with Erin. As I lay staring at the ceiling, thinking about the various ways I could get rid of her, I heard the same creaking noise. Raising my head, I saw the attic door had opened again. Stupid latch. Getting up slowly this time, I went over and closed it, pulling on the doorknob to see if it was latched this time. It seemed pretty solid – but something was still tickling at the fringes of my memory. I just couldn't quite grasp it.

When I got back in bed, I pulled the comforter over my shoulders. Lindsey was right. It seemed colder in here.

CHAPTER 11

I'd heard other people's descriptions of their out of body experiences, like they were hovering overhead and could see themselves, but felt like they weren't connected to their body. That was how I felt the next morning. I saw myself getting ready for school, eating breakfast and feeding Eby, but it's like I was watching it on TV. My limbs were moving and I spoke to my family, but my mind didn't seem to be registering any of it.

Since I was forbidden to drive for a few days – not really sure if that was the doc's rule or Mom's – Finn picked me up for school. "So, are those brain cells functioning properly yet?"

"If you're asking if my memory is back, the answer is still no, but Lindsey offered to help me remember when she dropped by yesterday to check on me," I said, glancing sideways to see Finn's reaction.

"Dude – she came over and you're just now telling me about it? Maybe you should get kicked in the head more often."

"I think she asked me out. She mentioned doing something after her concert this week."

"It's time to get serious, bro. You've got to get rid of Erin. She's like a rash that infects everyone she comes in contact with. There's just nothing good about her. Did you see her yesterday?"

"Haven't heard from her since Tuesday night at the hospital, when Mom kind of kicked her out. Even with a brain injury, yesterday was one of the best days I've had in months."

. . . . .

Sitting in classes was no different from this morning at home – I was there, but felt detached. My instructors asked questions and I'd want to answer, but it's like there was a wall between my thought processes and my mouth. The return of my headache was imminent.

"Cain, are you in there? Hello?"

"Should we take him to the nurse? This can't be good."

Voices. They sounded so distant. I knew it was Finn and Lindsey, but where were they? Then my head snapped up at the sound of Finn's hand slapping the cafeteria table directly in front of me.

"What was that for?" I shouted, the sharp sound echoing inside the walls of my head, increasing the strength of my headache.

"Cain, we've been trying to get your attention for the last ten minutes. You walked in here like you were in a trance, sat down, and started staring at the table in the corner. Since you weren't responding, Finn had to do something to get your attention," Lindsey said, glaring in Finn's direction.

Finn held up his hands in surrender. "It wasn't that loud and it worked, didn't it? What's up with you, Cain? I mean, look at your tray – it's all chick food."

Surveying my tray, I saw Finn was right. A salad, cottage cheese, some fruit. Not my usual burger and fries, pizza, or sub sandwich. Was cottage cheese actually a food? I must have looked like the poster child for massive confusion, because Lindsey seemed ready to haul me out of there.

"Cain, are you alright? Do you want me to take you to the nurse?"

"No, um….I'm okay. I just….." My head dropped as I raked my hands through my hair in frustration. "The last thing I remember is second period history this morning, and then now, when Finn smacked the table. Where was I in between?"

Finn shrugged. "This is the first time I've seen you since we got to school this morning, and you didn't drive, so there's no way you could have left campus."

"You don't remember any of your classes? Cain, that's a little scary. Are you sure you went to class? Do you see anyone close by you had a class with this morning?" Lindsey asked.

Scanning the few tables near us, I saw Ryan Shaw, a guy I sat beside in chemistry. "Hey, Ryan," I called, waving my hand to get his attention. "Was I in chemistry this morning?"

"You're asking me if you were in class? Is this another stupid joke of Finn's?"

"No, seriously. Just…was I in class or not?"

Ryan still looked skeptical. "Alright, yeah, Cain, you were there."

"Did I talk to you or do anything weird?"

"Weird? Like the way you finished our homework for tonight while Mr. Whay was still lecturing? Unless you suddenly developed mad skills in chemistry overnight, yeah, I'd say it was weird," Ryan said, turning back to his lunch.

I'd already done the chemistry homework? Usually it took me a couple of hours to complete it and that's only after I begged Finn for help. I should probably show it to him later to see if I'd known what I was doing.

"Since when do you understand chemistry and why have you been asking me for help all this time if you already knew how to do it? Well, at least we know you were in class. Now maybe you can explain why you ignored us and kept staring at the table with the football players," Finn said, tearing into his cheeseburger.

Shifting my attention to the table in the corner, I saw six varsity football players. I knew them, some better than others, but it's not like we hung out or were best bros or anything. As long as I could remember, there had always been a friendly, and sometimes not so friendly, rivalry between football players and soccer players. Why I'd been staring at them was as big a mystery to me as chemistry.

"Cain, maybe you should go home for the rest of the day. A memory lapse like this can't be good," Lindsey said, placing her hand over mine. If a pack of wild meerkats stormed through the cafeteria, there's no way I'd move right now.

I shook my head. "No, I'm good. Maybe it was just a side effect from the concussion, but I need to get something different for lunch, since what I have isn't edible," I said, wrinkling my nose at the pile of rabbit food on my tray. Cottage cheese, really?

"Just promise me you'll tell your mom about this when you get home, okay?" Lindsey asked, squeezing my hand. Behind her, Finn was giving me the thumbs up sign and waggling his eyebrows. Subtlety wasn't one of his strong suits.

"Sure. I'll tell her." All things considered, I guessed it was possible I might need to be checked again. Maybe things were still sloshing around in my head and hadn't settled back into place.

. . . . .

Since I hadn't been cleared yet for soccer practice, I had to sit and watch, but before dropping me off at home, Finn had checked my chemistry homework. Besides being an exceptional athlete, Finn was also kind of a genius and probably at the top of our class. You'd never know it by the way he acted sometimes, but chemistry was as easy for him as spewing out advice on my love life. By some miracle, all my homework was correct and as I got out of the car, I heard Finn mumbling something about smacking me in the head years ago if he'd have known it would make me smarter.

I hadn't had any more memory lapses this afternoon, so I didn't mention anything about it to Mom. The last thing she needed was to worry more about me. I felt fine. Stopping by the kitchen, I grabbed some yogurt and a banana and headed to my room for some PS4 time. Walking through the doorway, I noticed Eby lying on his back in a sunbeam on the floor, all four paws in the air. It was probably one of the only clear patches not littered with clothes or other debris.

Flinging my backpack onto my desk, I froze, not understanding what I was seeing. My yearbook from last year was lying open, and some pages had been ripped out. Several were shredded, littering the floor, and some were strewn across the desk. Knowing I wasn't to blame for this, I looked over to Eby, wondering if he was responsible. But he'd been declawed when we'd adopted him and the possibility of him shredding papers was impossible. Chewing, maybe, he seemed to have an oral fixation sometimes, but shredding? No way.

Picking up the bigger chunks of what was left, I saw some of the same faces from the corner cafeteria table staring back at me. The football players. The ones I'd been watching at lunch and had no idea why.

Chapter 12

"So now you hate the football team? Is it football in general or just our players specifically?"

"You're still an ass, Finn," I said, enjoying the warm breeze blowing through the open window of the car as we drove to school. "What if this is serious? Why would I suddenly hate football players? I don't remember ripping up my yearbook, but I'm also missing two or three hours from yesterday morning and two days from earlier this week. Maybe I did it."

"Did you tell your mom about yesterday? The missing hours?"

Focusing on my backpack, I began fumbling with one of the straps and shrugged. "I guess I forgot."

"You forgot. After finding what was either the aftermath of your declawed cat on a paper rampage or you blacking out again and having a raging hate for football players. Erin, a girlfriend you can't stand, and someone who clearly needs therapy to break her mirror obsession – still dating her. Blackouts and memory lapses after a head injury. Do you tell your mom? No. What do these things have in common? You're an avoider, Cain."

"An avoider? Is that even a word?"

"That's what you are, so it must be a word. I can almost understand the thing with Erin since you hate hurting anyone's feelings. Geez, you even dodge butterflies when you're driving. But your health? That's just dangerous, my friend, and if you don't tell your mom, I will. Got it?"

Okay, maybe I'd always tended to avoid situations that could potentially go off the rails, being more of a go with the flow kind of guy. But if there were complications from the concussion, getting things taken care of sooner rather than later was the safest and smartest option.

"Yeah, I got it."

He sighed, "Alright. I've got your back, you've got mine, right?"

"Always."

．　．　．　．　．

"Cain, you jerk, are you listening to me? What's your problem? How could you do that to me?"

I gradually became aware of Erin standing in front of me and yelling, her pink-clawed fists punching at my arms and chest. Instinctively, I grabbed her wrists to make her stop.

"Erin, what are you doing?"

"What am I doing?" she screeched. "I've been standing here screaming at you for the past five minutes and you haven't even looked at me until now! How could you humiliate me like that in front of everyone? Who do you think you are to speak to me that way?"

Clouds of confusion drifted in my mind and I had no idea what Erin was talking about. Now aware of my surroundings, I heard the crash of helmets and the grunts of players as they were tackled. I'd been standing by the bleachers at the football field during their team practice. The last thing I remembered was going to my locker after physics, right before biology class. The class I had with Erin. I'd blacked out again.

"You're lucky I dated you, Cain, because I'm obviously out of your league. I thought I could make you into someone worthy of being with me and look how you treated me! I hope you shrivel up and die!" The sharp crack of her hand across my cheek drowned out the crash of helmets on the field. Rubbing the spot where I'm sure Erin had left a handprint, I wondered if those pink claws had scratched a little too – it really stung.

"Sweetheart, trust me when I say someday you'll look back on this and realize how wrong you were and how desperately you needed to adjust your priorities in life. Get some help."

My head snapped up at the sound of Finn's voice, just in time to see Erin flip him off before crossing the parking lot.

"Cain, what are you doing here? I've been looking for you the past hour when you didn't meet me at the car," Finn said, stretching out on the bleachers in the late afternoon sun.

"It happened again. I don't remember anything after physics and I woke up here to Erin hitting me and screaming. What did I do to her?"

"You're saying you don't remember having a very public breakup with Erin in the hall after biology class? Dude, it was epic. Everyone's talking about it. I don't know when I've been prouder of you," Finn said, wiping a fake tear from his eye.

Learning from others about what I'd done was like hearing stories of someone else's life. "I broke up with her?"

"Broke up with her? Cain, you decimated her. You told her what a horrible person she was – shallow, narcissistic, snobbish, and seriously lacking in intelligence. I never knew you understood such big words. You also told her all the designer clothes and makeup in the world would never make her into something she's not and to stay away from you for good."

Holy crap. I'd said that? I mean, it wasn't a lie – that's how I felt about her, but saying it in public, in a hallway full of students, was never the way I'd have handled it – consciously, I mean. However it had happened, I should probably celebrate. The wicked witch was dead.

"The last time I remember seeing Erin, other than just now, was in bio class yesterday and she was ignoring me, probably still waiting for me to apologize about what happened at the hospital."

"And you're here, at the football field, after blacking out again. Are you telling your mom or am I?"

I sighed. "How about we both talk to her."

. . . .

They were coming for me - so close I could almost feel their breath on the back of my neck. I knew what would happen if they caught me, knew things wouldn't end well for me. Had to get away. Running. Out of breath. Chest was hurting. Couldn't look back. Needed to know – had to see how close they were. *Don't look back.* Glanced over my shoulder.

Tripped over something. No! Falling. Couldn't let them get me. So close. The door was just ahead. Needed to keep moving, but still falling down, so far down. Then darkness – everywhere - all around me. Pinned. Couldn't move my arms or legs. Struggled to breath. No air. Pressure on my chest. Turned my head side to side - searching for air. Please, not like this, please. Someone - *help me*. Couldn't breathe. *HELP ME!*

"Cain, sweetie, it's time to get ready for your appointment. Are you awake?"

I jerked upright in bed, gasping for breath, sucking in oxygen to fill my aching lungs. The feeling of being suffocated, unable to move and alone in the darkness clung to me and I didn't understand where I was.

"Cain, are you alright? It's me – it's Mom. You're just having a nightmare."

She spoke to me in a soft tone, one hand rubbing my back as the other held my hand. "Don't touch me!" I shouted, pushing her away.

She drew back, but spoke calmly. "You need to wake up, it's alright."

My gaze swept the room, looking for the threat, searching for whatever – or whoever – had been chasing me. But all I saw was Eby sprawled out in the morning sun beaming through my windows. Home. I was in my own bed, safe. I fell back to the pillow, my hand covering my eyes as I tried to calm my breathing.

"That must have been some nightmare," Mom said. I felt the mattress dip as she sat on the edge of my bed.

"You have no idea."

"Well, you need to get ready for your appointment. I'll have breakfast ready for you in about fifteen minutes, so get to it."

After talking to Mom about my losses of time, she'd immediately called the doctor's office. When I'd been discharged a couple of days ago, the doctor had told both of us I could still have some memory lapses over the next week, something that was entirely normal, but just to be safe, she wanted me to come in for another CT.

Groaning, I pulled the covers up over my head. I probably hadn't slept more than a couple of hours last night.

"Cain?"

"I'm up. I'm awake, Mom." Throwing off the covers, I dragged my weary body to a sitting position.

"We'll leave in thirty minutes. Don't fall asleep again."

"Got it." The nightmare had seemed so real, I could still feel the darkness pressing in and couldn't get enough air. But the strangest part was that even though it had been me in the nightmare, it hadn't been me. I was a teenage girl – how insane was that?

· · · · ·

"So the doctor isn't worried about your memory lapses? Everything's alright?"

"I had another CT done and everything looked okay, other than the concussion. She said it's probably just a side effect of the injury, but if it keeps happening, they may want to do further tests." I'd practically tackled people in the hallway trying to get to English lit a little early so I could talk with Lindsey.

"Well, that's a relief. I heard about your epic breakup with Erin. I guess that's one good thing that came of your memory lapses," Lindsey said, one side of her mouth turned up.

Ducking my head, I nervously twisted the ring on my finger. "Um, yeah, that wasn't my style. I mean, I'm glad to be rid of her, but I never would have done anything like that, you know, embarrassed her that way."

"So you really don't think she's a total waste of molecules that sucks the happiness out of life itself?"

"Seriously? I said that?"

"Yeah – I caught that last bit when I was coming out of calculus. So you're saying that's not accurate?"

Raising my head, I saw a teasing glint in her eye. "Honestly, that's a pretty good description of how I feel about Erin."

Before I could say more, Ms. Brody started class. "Alright, to brighten your day, we're having a pop quiz over chapters five through ten this morning."

"We'll talk later," Lindsey mouthed silently. I couldn't wait.

. . . . . .

"So I heard Erin's slobbering over the football team captain now," Finn said, taking out my guy in Fallout 4 and making my gamer chair vibrate.

The past couple of days had been near perfect. I'd gotten through the weekend with no memory lapses and Lindsey's concert was Tuesday night. Finn and I were hanging out in my room playing PS4 after a light soccer practice in the backyard. The doc hadn't cleared me to play, but that wasn't going to keep me from kicking around the soccer ball when I could.

"Don't put those images in my head, bro. My brain's still sloshing around and I don't need to fill it with crap like that. Nice shirt. New?" Today's shirt read 'Wands Don't Kill Wizards, Wizards Kill Wizards.'

"You like? It's true, you know. There's no reason wands should be outlawed, it's the wizard that makes the choice to use it for evil instead of good, right? Support their right to carry, I say. Are you with me, Cain?"

"Sure. I see no reason why wizards shouldn't be able to carry their wands. You have my full support and I'll sign any petition you'd like."

We continued playing and our trash talking each other would have sent Mom into hysterics, but it's guy code. You gotta do it.

Out of the corner of my eye, behind Finn, I saw some movement, thinking it was Eby again. He'd been bringing Finn cat toys all afternoon and even curled up on his lap once. But it wasn't Eby. The attic door was opening on its own. "Okay, that's a little freaky."

"What?" Finn asked, pausing the game.

"That," I said, nodding towards the attic door. "The way it creeped open, I half expected someone to walk out. Eby didn't go up there, did he?"

"Um, yeah. Cain, we need to talk," he said, putting down the controller. "I hadn't mentioned anything because I didn't want to upset you with the concussion and all, but you've forgotten some pretty eventful things that happened in your room last week."

"No, dude, it opened like that when Lindsey was here the other day. I guess the latch is loose or something. Maybe I need to get a screwdriver. If it keeps opening like that, my room will turn into a sauna with the heat from upstairs," I said, getting up from the gamer chair.

"Trust me, a screwdriver isn't going to fix the attic door. I was hoping you'd remember on your own, but I guess that's not happening. Cain, your room is ....."

Before he could finish, several things happened at once. A rush of cold air swept down the attic stairs and exploded into the room, hitting me like a giant wave. Then a mini tornado formed, a swirling vortex sucking in loose papers and protein bar wrappers from the floor by Finn, rising five feet into the air, the wind blasting his hair straight back from his forehead.

And everything I'd forgotten - the blood found in a corner of the attic, the camcorder being thrown across the room, writing in the condensation on the bathroom mirror - came crashing back, and I let out a gasp of recognition.

The ghost of Sarah Butler lived in my attic.

CHAPTER 13

As the funnel dissipated and papers whirled back to the floor, Finn and I gaped at each other, his shocked expression mirroring my own. "Now do you see why a screwdriver won't do you any good?"

I heard him, but my mind was preoccupied clicking things into slots, replacing the empty spaces with memories from last week – the coldness in the attic, the certainty someone had been sitting on my bed while I was half asleep, the conversation I'd had with Mom about Sarah's blood found in the attic. The video. The video! The face glaring at the camcorder! I remembered everything.

"Cain, did you hear me? Are you blacking out again? Shannon?" Finn snapped his fingers in front of my face in an effort to get my attention, then grabbed my shoulder and shook it.

"Get off me, Finn," I said, shoving him away. "Yes, I saw that and I remember everything. Sarah's ghost is living in my attic and wants our attention."

"You think? Before your concussion, we'd planned on trying to make contact with her. Do you think she's here right now?"

Making contact with a spirit had always seemed slightly hair-raising, but kind of fascinating on television. But fascination didn't really describe my current state of mind, thinking that the ghost of a dead teenage girl could be here, watching us right now. Skirting the edge of panic was a better description.

"Um….I'm not sure," I said, my voice wavering slightly. "It doesn't feel as cold to me now. Isn't the cold supposed to mean she's here?"

"Why should I know? I never read the ghost etiquette book. But you're right – it doesn't feel unnaturally cold. Maybe she did that so we wouldn't forget about her, or to help you remember."

"Well, it worked," I replied, laughing nervously. "It all came back. So what now?"

"Maybe it's as simple as asking Sarah what's next. Should we try?"

Dad had always said if you have a problem, work on a solution. Don't wait around and expect it to resolve on its own. Action instead of inaction. "I guess it's worth a shot. Sarah? Are you here?"

Silence. Finn eyes flitted around the room, ducking his head slightly as if he expected someone – or something – to swoop overhead. When dealing with the unknown, it was a valid response.

"Would you like to talk to us? We don't want to hurt you, but it seems like you've been trying to get our attention and we're ready to listen." Then Eby came bounding into the room and dropped a fuzzy ball in front of Finn in hopes of playing fetch, one of his favorite games.

"Based on his previous reactions, if Eby's here, Sarah's not," I said, watching as he pawed at Finn's leg, reminding him the ball was waiting.

Finn exhaled loudly, picking up the ball and tossing it across the room as Eby pounced after it, scattering the papers from the earlier mini funnel cloud. "I don't know if I should be frustrated or relieved. But I'm thinking relieved. Are we ready for this?"

"You really think we have a choice?"

. . . . . .

Jolting awake, I lay in bed trying to pinpoint what woke me. Maybe it was the loud thudding in my chest or heavy breathing, but I wasn't sure why I felt this way. A nightmare maybe? I didn't remember dreaming anything. The attic door was closed, and my hand slid down to the spot where Eby usually slept beside me, but his warm furry body wasn't there. Lying on my back, I stared at the ceiling, the darkness broken only by moonlight streaming through the window and the dim, orange glow of the street lamp outside. The house was quiet, but maybe a noise that didn't belong in the stillness of the early morning hours woke me - Eby running through the hall or a book sliding off the desk and falling to the floor.

I rose to my elbows, peering into the shadows, searching for the possible source of a noise, but it was a useless effort in the controlled chaos of my room. I'd never be able to tell if anything had fallen – I probably had more things on the floor than on my desk or dresser. After listening for a couple of minutes and nothing disturbing the silence, I lay back down, convinced it was probably Eby. Anything lying on a horizontal surface seemed to offend him and he took pleasure in knocking things to the floor.

Mind made up, I rolled to my side, away from the window, and pulled the comforter over my shoulder, hoping to fall back asleep. I was drifting, hovering in that hazy area where you're aware of your surroundings, but one foot is already in the dream world, when I heard the soft creak of the attic door directly behind me. And just like that, I was ripped from the dream world and tossed back to reality.

A reality that consisted of a ghost revealing herself to me.

I inhaled deeply in an attempt to calm my breathing and reminded myself making contact with a ghost was something I'd always wanted. Ideas that had seemed exciting and cool in the light of day could take on a whole new definition in the dark of the night.

Then, to my left, I felt the mattress dip slightly at the foot of the bed, as if someone had sat down.

Squeezing my eyes tightly shut, I dug deep for the courage to turn and see if she was sitting at the end of the bed. Because I was warm-natured, the comforter from my knees down had been kicked to the side and I remembered the cardinal rule of childhood – never leave body parts out from under the covers because everyone knew the monsters under the bed considered that fair game. I was wishing I'd carried this rule into my early adult years, when I felt a feather-light touch on my left calf.

Icy tendrils rushed from my calf to my scalp, the soft touch much cooler than the room temperature. The parts of my body still beneath the comforter were covered with goosebumps, but not from the frigid touch of whatever waited for me. It was time to take action.

Squaring my jaw and taking a deep breath, I rolled slowly away from the wall, brushing strands of hair away from my face.

And there she was, bright moonlight streaming through her partially transparent body.

There was no doubt in my mind who she was. I'd seen her picture in my year book, the online newspaper, and her face glaring into the camera lens on the video. The silvery, shimmering ghost of Sarah Butler was sitting at the foot of my bed, her ebony eyes boring into me.

CHAPTER 14

I remembered reading somewhere that self-preservation may be the strongest instinct in humans. And mine kicked in with the speed of a freight train. Jerking away from Sarah, I attempted to leap from the bed, but the upper half of my body slammed to the floor, my legs tangled in the blankets. Frantically kicking at them, I wriggled free, then flipped over and scuttled backwards like a crab, away from the bed and away from Sarah.

Not exactly the reaction I'd envisioned when meeting a spirit from the other side.

My back hit the wall beneath the window and there was nowhere to go. The attic door was to my right, my bathroom and the hallway to my left. Unfortunately, the last two options required me to go past Sarah, and I wasn't ready for that.

Was I scared of her? My trembling hands were a good indication, but I wondered if it was more fear of the unknown rather than Sarah. I wasn't sure if this encounter would be friendly, like when Harry Potter saw his parents, or more along the lines of the girl that crawled from the well and left a trail of carnage behind her. A magic wand right about now sure would have been helpful.

Sarah shifted slightly on the bed, turning to face me as I pushed further back against the wall, knees drawn up to my chin, arms wrapped around my legs. Every muscle was tensed, my breathing heavy and with every exhale, my breath hung in the arctic air that came with Sarah's presence.

She cocked her head to one side, solid black eyes contemplating me, as if she were confused. Maybe she was confused about being here. In one movie I'd seen, Bruce Willis's character didn't realize he was a ghost. Maybe it was the same for Sarah. If that was true, she probably didn't understand why I was reacting this way.

Sarah's hand gently rose from the bed and extended in my direction, as if she was reaching for me, but there was no way I'd move closer until I understood her intentions. I studied her, like I evaluated opponents on the soccer field, but at least their motives were a known quantity. Sarah was still a big question mark.

It was impossible for me to be any closer to the wall than I already was, but that didn't stop me from trying, slowly shaking my head, letting her know I wouldn't come to her. Her face contorted into an expression of – sadness? Was that even possible? Sarah lowered her hand back to the bed, her head following. She looked miserable, and her filmy body collapsed into itself as if defeated.

My mouth seemed bone dry, but I swallowed nervously, the noise deafening in the silent room. Why was she here? What did she want? Questions needed to be asked, but I didn't know if my voice would even work. Taking a shaky deep breath, I clasped my arms even tighter around my knees.

"Wh...why are you h-h-here?" I stammered, my voice high, more the pitch of a ten-year-old girl.

Sarah's head snapped up, and as she raised her hand again, reaching towards me, she began to fade. When she'd first appeared, although semi-transparent, her shape and features had been distinct, but Sarah now seemed to lose clarity, the hazy lines of her arms and legs blurring together until only a faint mist was visible.

And then she was gone.

My limbs refused to move as I continued staring at the spot where Sarah had been, my eyes unblinking. Either I'd stopped breathing or the room temperature had returned to normal because I couldn't see my breath anymore, but the warmth had no effect on me. My body felt chilled from the outside, the coldness seeping layer by layer through to my bones.

Before she'd disappeared, before her facial features became unrecognizable and blurred into a filmy vapor, Sarah had looked at me, her expression pleading, almost as if she was desperate for my help.

• • • • • •

"Cain, why are you sleeping on the floor with trash and stinky clothes and soccer shoes?"

My eyelids strained open to see Maddie standing over me, hands on her hips, looking around my room with the expression of someone who'd had a skunk stuck up her nose.

"If you're saying my room smells, I get it. Do you need something, Maddie?" I pushed myself to a sitting position, but not without difficulty. My body felt heavy, as if I hadn't slept in days.

"You're late. Mom said to wake you because Finn will be here soon to get you. Why are you sleeping on the floor anyway?"

"Um....I fell asleep here after gaming last night. Did someone feed Eby?" Struggling to stand, I leaned against the wall for support.

"I did," she said, kicking at an empty Gatorade bottle. "I tried to share my cereal with him again, but Mom said I had to stop. I don't know why, 'cause Eby really likes cereal."

In spite of my body aches and the swirling confusion of last night's events, Maddie's words made me snicker. "Yeah, I can't argue with you on that one, but Mom's right. You can't keep sharing a spoon with him." My goal was to get to the restroom, but it seemed a mile away instead of six feet to my left. Pushing off from the wall, I attempted to head in that direction, but stumbled and had to grab the wall again to steady myself.

"So I'll get Eby his own spoon. Are you sick, Cain? Should I get Mom?"

"No, I'm fine, Maddie, just give me a minute. I'm a little stiff from sleeping on the floor." I let go of the wall, determined to stand on my own. Once I grabbed a shower and let the hot water loosen up my aching muscles, I was sure I'd feel more like myself. After last night, this was probably my body's delayed reaction to the shock. I hoped, anyway.

Shuffling a few inches at a time, I made my way toward the shower. "See? I'm fine."

"Okay, if you're sure," she said, turning and skipping out of the room, oblivious to the freakish activities that had been going on across the house from her bedroom. Everything in Maddie's world was rainbows, as it should be, and would stay that way if I had anything to say about it. Then I stopped cold in my tracks as a terrifying thought crossed my mind. What if Sarah wasn't confined to the attic and my bedroom?

.   .   .   .   .

"I saw her last night, Finn. Sarah. She was sitting at the end of my bed and just about scared the crap out of me." Palm trees swayed in the morning breeze and Finn and I had forgone the A/C, choosing to roll down the windows instead as he drove us to school.

"Don't take a swing at me or anything – remember, I'm driving and I literally hold your life in my hands right now, but could you have been dreaming? I mean, it's possible, you know."

I wouldn't lie and say that thought hadn't crossed my mind this morning, but when I was drying off after my shower, I knew without a doubt that wasn't the case. "I'm positive. Where Sarah touched my leg last night, she left a bruise in the shape of a handprint."

Finn was silent, squinting into the early morning sun. He was never quiet for this long.

"Waiting."

"For?"

"Your thoughts. I say a ghost was at the foot of my bed last night, left a bruise on my leg and you've got nothing to say about it? How about something like, 'Geez, Cain, are you alright?' You know, show a little concern, dude."

Finn laid his hand atop the console between us, palm up. "Well?" he asked, glancing over at me before shifting his gaze back to the road.

"What?"

"Don't you want to hold my hand? You're being kind of needy right now, and that's the best I can do."

I shoved his hand back to his lap. Mom said sometimes Finn and I sounded like an old married couple and although I'd laughed it off, now I thought it might not be out of the realm of possibility.

"Seriously, could you possibly have been dreaming and bruised your leg yourself? You know, squeezing it while dreaming, imagining it was her?" he asked.

"I couldn't have made the handprint myself. It's too small to be my own. So what else you got?"

Finn's left arm was propped against the door as he ran his hand through his hair, making it stick up even more than it usually did.

"Well?"

"Maybe there's not a logical explanation. We saw her on the video, you saw her last night, so we know she's there. Did it hurt when she bruised you?"

Getting out of the car in the school parking lot, I slung my backpack over my shoulder. "No. That's another strange thing. When she touched me, it was feather light, but cold. Maybe I was so panicked I just didn't notice. My heart can't take being woken up like that every night, so we've got to try talking to her again. Either she goes all exorcist on me and spews green crap out of her mouth, or she tells me why she needs help. Maybe she wants me to contact her parents or something."

Finn pressed the remote button, locking the car behind us. "How could you even begin to have a conversation like that with her parents? There's no way they'd believe you. With your concussion, they'd throw you back in the hospital for sure. Bet there's an opening on the psych ward."

"Yeah, I'd come across as delusional," I sighed, opening the door to the main hallway of the school. "Why don't you come over this evening after practice and we'll try to contact her again."

"I know what you're thinking. If she goes all exorcist, you can push me in front of you, save yourself and run. But you know I'm all about new experiences. Maybe I'll be able to cross helping a damsel ghost in distress off my bucket list."

. . . . .

"Seriously, Cain, what kind of pervy fixation do you have for these football players? Or is it just a fetish for sweaty male athletes in general, because if that's the case, it might explain some of the looks you've given me over the years."

Finn's words sounded distant, almost like he was behind a door talking to me. Damn. It had happened again. I'd blacked out and wandered over to the football field, watching the team while they practiced. After a weekend with no lost time, I'd thought I was past this.

"You did it again, didn't you? You had no idea you were here until you heard me, right?"

"Yeah," I replied, rubbing my face. "Let's just go home, alright?"

"You're sure you're okay?" Finn asked, searching my face.

I nodded. "Let's go. And for the record, no, I don't have a fetish for sweaty male athletes and even if I did, it wouldn't be your backside I'd be staring at."

"You should be so lucky. Prime choice Grade A right here, sweetheart," he said, slapping his behind.

CHAPTER 15

"So, just asking her to come out didn't work last time. Do we need a Ouija board? Maybe a medium?"

Googling 'how to contact a ghost' brought up over fifteen million results, but we still hadn't agreed on the way to start. "How would I know, Finn? It's not like I've done this before."

"Well, how about we start in the attic, you know, in the corner that was so cold, where you saw the blood. That seems kind of logical, right?"

Finn might have said he lived for new experiences, but neither of us was too anxious to be the first up the stairway, and after losing two out of three rounds of rock, paper, scissors, that honor fell to me. When we realized we were tip-toeing instead of walking normally, our nervous laughter lightened the situation a little, although once we reached the top of the stairs, both of us stood there, peering into the cloaked, hidden corners of the attic, sweat rolling down our foreheads.

"So, which corner is the cold one?"

"The left side in the back," I said, pointing past the stacks of dusty moving boxes.

"Of course it would be in the back. In the darkest corner. The longest way from the door. The only way out of here if everything goes off the rails. Lead the way," Finn said, releasing a heavy sigh.

The single overhead bulb didn't illuminate much so, armed with the additional flashlight app on our phones, we inched toward the far corner. Finn kept peeking around some of the boxes like he thought Sarah was going to jump out at him. Then again, maybe she would. How was I to know? She'd left bruises on my leg last night, so who's to say she wouldn't try to do something worse to us? I was really beginning to question my sanity and wondered what had made me think this was a good idea.

I honestly didn't know how we were going to do this. Just because I'd seen others communicate with ghosts on television didn't mean I was qualified on my own. Last night's attempts hadn't gotten me anywhere.

"Feels like the same temperature back here as it does over there – inferno level. Should we sit down? Chant or something?"

"Again, Finn, why do you think I know the standard protocol for summoning a ghost?" I asked, now more irritated than nervous, wiping sweat from my face.

"Well, she seems to like you, so maybe she'll just show up since you're here," he snapped.

"Or maybe you'll scare her away. You tend to have that effect on women sometimes."

"Really." Finn crossed his arms over his chest. "Well, I don't see a trail of babes following you around, bro, so you've got no reason to talk. You still don't have the cojones to ask Lindsey out."

"I don't have to because she asked me out, and the only woman I've seen you with lately is my Mom. Wait – scratch that. Way too disturbing."

"At least I can…." Finn stopped abruptly, his eyes widening. "Cain, why can I see your breath when you talk?"

And that's when I felt it. While we'd been talking smack to each other, the air had turned bitter cold, like we were standing in a meat locker, not an attic with a temperature in the upper nineties.

Sarah was here.

Finn's widened eyes threatened to pop out of his head as they flitted around the attic, looking for her. I wasn't any better, wiping my sweaty palms on my shorts, breathing heavily as if I'd just run up the stairs.

"Sss…Sarah? Are you h-h-here?" I stuttered. I got no response, but the wintry air encasing us whipped around our legs, the scattered dust motes swirling into a miniature funnel cloud.

"Try again," Finn whispered.

I licked my lips nervously. "I think you might need some help. Is that true? Can you answer us?"

Maybe it was from the cold or because I was spooked, but I felt the darkness closing in, my legs quivered like jello, and I stumbled toward Finn. He caught my arm and draped it around his neck, tucked the phone in his shorts and wrapped his other arm around my waist, while I leaned heavily against him.

"Cain, are you alright? Do we need to go back downstairs?"

"No. No, I'm good. Just felt dizzy for a minute."

Finn's gaze was fixed over my shoulder and I could see the short bursts of his breath in the air. I felt his arm tense. "She's here," he whispered, so softly I barely heard him.

Still leaning on Finn, I turned slowly in the direction of his unwavering stare. Was it possible to both dread something, yet still be so curious you wanted it to happen? That's the way I felt. Unsure of Sarah's reaction – she'd already injured me once - I was still somewhat giddy at the thought of talking to her. The fanboy in me who loved horror movies was dying to see what would happen. Um, maybe that wasn't the best word choice.

Aside from being dead and not of this world, Sarah was kind of awesome. Her shape was still slightly unfocused and fuzzy, hair flickering between silvery white and a lighter brown color, and her eyes reflected the cold glint of steel. Remembering how she'd looked last night, I'd swear she seemed more solid, because I couldn't see all the way through to the wall behind her.

"Do you want to hurt us?" I asked softly. Her brow furrowed as she shook her head in a small movement. The room spun slightly and I must have leaned too far to one side, because I felt Finn pull me in closer.

"Sarah, do you need help?" Finn asked, his voice huskier than normal.

She slowly nodded in response.

"Can you talk?" I asked. Until now, the way Sarah would sound, if she could talk, had never occurred to me. Would her voice even resemble a human's? Maybe it would be gravelly, like her throat was full of dirt. Recalling how some of those possessed people in horror movies sounded, I thought it might be too much to handle if she sounded like any of them.

"Yes, I can talk." Normal - a little hushed, but completely normal.

"Why are you here?" I asked. Although it looked like Finn and I were in no danger from Sarah, we kept our distance. Just in case.

"I died in this house while it was being built." Well, that answered one question. Sarah knew she was dead.

"We figured it was something like that. They found traces of your blood here in the attic. Tell us what we can do to help you, because I gotta say, you've really been creeping me out, appearing in my bedroom at night, opening the attic door, freaking out my cat."

"What do you need from us, Sarah?" Finn asked. "Because we don't know what to say right now. I mean, did you not go to the light? Do you want us to get a message to your parents? Have unfinished business?"

The glow surrounding her glimmered brighter. "I guess you could say I have some unfinished business. I was killed here and need your help to make my murderers pay for what they did to me."

CHAPTER 16

Finding murderers and making them pay? Not the answer we'd expected. After the initial shock, when I found my voice again, I asked, "Um, how could we do that, Sarah? How could we prove to the police you were murdered?"

"Do you know who did it? Do you remember what happened?" Finn asked.

Sarah surged in our direction, closing the distance between us. "Of course I know who did it! I remember every detail about the night I died!" Sarah snapped, her face a mask of fury, hair snaking in different directions.

Finn and I staggered backwards, with him still supporting me, both of us unnerved at the sudden change in her demeanor. If someone told me right now Sarah was possessed, I'd have no trouble believing them.

Whatever Sarah saw in our faces made her back off and take the anger level down a couple of notches, gradually floating back to her original position. Putting some distance between us again made me think her outburst wasn't meant to intimidate us, only her emotions getting out of control. She'd been murdered here – I'd be harboring some anger too. But my body was poised to run at a moment's notice if it happened again.

"Can you tell us what happened?" I asked. "Do you even want to talk about it?"

Sarah looked toward the window, an expression of sadness washing over her. "I'll tell you what I can. My energy is fading, so I don't know how much longer I can stay. I wasn't the popular type in high school, guys weren't falling over themselves to ask me out, but if you needed a good grade, you wanted to be my lab partner in chemistry or copy my calculus homework. And I was okay with that. Grades were my way out of here and I'd already been offered scholarships to some good colleges, away from my overly strict parents and those shallow people at school who never thought about life

82

beyond those walls. A campus where there were more people like me. Maybe I was naïve to think that way, but it had to be better than high school."

Finn and I looked each other and nodded in silent agreement. Neither of us remembered much about Sarah, but she was right about the cliques at school. Like you needed to belong to one of them to validate your existence, and I could understand her wanting to get away from here and start over.

"Everything changed in early March this year. Three guys, the type who'd never looked twice in my direction, started talking to me in class, complimenting me on my clothes, even asking me to their parties. At first, I ignored them. Why would they pay any attention to me and why would I care if they did?

"I kept waiting for them to tell me what they really wanted, like getting me to do their homework or copy off my tests. But they never asked for anything, and I stupidly started to believe maybe I was enough, that they really liked me. They convinced me to go to a party at a house under construction and said a lot of people would be there, promising I'd have fun if I went.

"I let myself get excited, thinking maybe I'd misjudged these guys and would really get to experience high school before graduation. But when we got here that night, it was only the four of us, and they said the others were out picking up beer and snacks and would be here soon."

The expression on Finn's face told me we were thinking the same thing. No one else had been coming for a party. Feeling stronger now, I was able to stand on my own and move away from Finn.

"You're probably wondering how I could have been so trusting, why I believed them, and I've asked myself that a million times. But the part of me that was so excited guys might actually find me attractive ignored the rational part of me that knew better."

"Did they rape you?" Finn asked softly. I dreaded hearing the answer to that question, hoping so much it would be no. Sarah looked down before answering and I was afraid I already knew the answer.

"No, they didn't rape me, but that might have been part of their plan. I have to stop now, I'm getting weaker."

While listening intently to her, I hadn't noticed Sarah was fading and could now easily see through her to the wall behind. "Wait! Sarah, before you go, can you tell us who did this to you?"

Sarah spat out their identities as if she'd bitten into rotten food, and the echo of their names was all that was left of Sarah as she dissolved. "Jacob Headley, Nathan Nivens, and Liam Brooks." And then she was gone.

We stared at each other, speechless, stunned at Sarah's revelation. Finn and I knew all three of these guys - not well, but we definitely knew who they were. They were in our senior class.

"Football players," Finn stated, his voice flat.

. . . . . .

"Come on, Cain, you don't see a correlation at all?" Finn asked, eyebrows raised in disbelief.

We were at our favorite pizza place, a half-eaten, extra-large pepperoni, mushroom, and black olive pizza on the table between us, discussing what Sarah had told us. Not much comes between teenage boys and their appetites. "Okay, maybe, but I don't see how it would be possible."

"I've found you at the football field twice now, staring at the players, and you have no memory of why or how you got there. You were dazed and confused while leering at them during lunch in the cafeteria. You're a borderline stalker, my friend," he said, taking a large bite of pizza, leaving a string of cheese dangling from his mouth.

"So you're saying I somehow subconsciously knew these guys murdered Sarah and that's why I've been so fixated on them?"

Finn swallowed, then slurped up the dangling cheese. "Hang on, dude. We don't know for sure they murdered her. Maybe they were just responsible for getting her there and then something else happened to her. We have to wait to hear the rest of her story."

Rubbing my face, I nodded. "You're right. This is serious and I shouldn't be making assumptions before I know everything. So, what are you trying to say about me being a stalker?"

Reaching for the pizza, Finn grabbed his fifth piece. "Try to stay with me on this and keep the brain cells still remaining open to ideas, alright? What if Sarah was somehow able to take over your body and mind? Control your actions so you don't remember what happened when she was inside your head."

"What? You think I wasn't in control of my own body and mind? That's the stupidest thing I've ever heard. How could Sarah even be in my body?" Finn's idea seemed ridiculous, but a small voice in the back of my mind said it wasn't completely outer limits. And that made me very nervous and more than a little scared.

"What about your epic breakup with Erin? You didn't remember any of that and the way you did it in front of everyone, the things you said to her, that's just not your style, Cain. But those words could easily have come from someone who'd been treated like a second class citizen by people like Erin, right? Just think about it.

"Obviously we don't know the rules and regulations about ghosts and what they can and can't do. Up until a couple of hours ago, I wasn't even sure I believed in them. It's a whole gray area, so who knows what's possible? Maybe we need to find someone who can help us with this."

I wadded my napkin into a ball and tossed it on the table. "Like who?"

"Ghost tours are a booming market in this city. There have to be some psychics and mediums out there for the tourists. Some of them may even be legitimate."

"You know where to find one of those?"

He shrugged. "Can't be that hard. I'm on it."

CHAPTER 17

While I lay in bed that night, I kept thinking about Finn's idea of Sarah using my body as a puppet to do her bidding. Then I thought about how I'd suddenly felt weak sometimes and wondered if she was siphoning off my energy. Didn't ghosts need energy to appear? Sarah certainly made it sound like she did. Then again, I had a head injury and the weakness could just be a side effect, but I was definitely going to pay more attention to when I felt that way and see if there was any correlation.

The more I thought about it, the more uneasy I felt, so I decided to spend the night on the couch downstairs again. If anyone asked, I'd say I just fell asleep in front of the TV. Wouldn't be the first time.

• • • • •

Erin was still avoiding me at school – no complaints here, but I still felt a little guilty about how the breakup had happened. Finn had been right. When all my memories came gushing back, I remembered all the horrible things I'd said to her and the look of humiliation on her face as students gathered around us and watched, probably uploading it to YouTube. Although I had the memory of breaking up with her, it's like I was watching another person. It was me, but not me. Which would support Finn's theory about Sarah invading my body.

All thoughts of Erin were eclipsed when Lindsey walked into English lit class. Seeing her made me feel as if electricity had shot through my brain – among other places, and my cheeks flushed in embarrassment at that thought as she took her seat next to mine.

"You're still coming to the concert tonight, right Cain?"

"Definitely. Wouldn't miss it." Something just moved in my stomach. Did I have butterflies? Maybe it was just gas. Okay, didn't want to think about all the ways I could be embarrassed if that was the case.

"Awesome! How about we grab some burgers after? That new place down from the concert hall has amazing double bacon cheeseburgers."

"Sounds good to me. They're my favorite."

"I know," she said, reaching over and trailing her fingers down my forearm.

I could die a happy man right about now.

. . . . .

The concert hall was more crowded than I'd expected. I assumed the audience consisted of parents of the musicians and their siblings who were forced to attend, but also boyfriends and girlfriends. Or boyfriend-wannabes, like me.

"Did she compel you to come or are you here to impress my sister in hopes of getting into her pants?"

Caleb, Lindsey's brother and my teammate on the soccer team, stood in the aisle next to me, arms crossed over his chest, looking as if he would launch an attack if I moved an inch.

"What? No! Geez, Caleb, calm down. I'm here because Lindsey asked me to come and I wanted to hear her play."

Caleb glowered at me a moment longer, as if he was still searching for ulterior motives.

"Take a seat if you want, but quit looking at me like that. I'd never disrespect Lindsey. She's amazing and I'd never treat her that way."

Maybe he believed me or gave me the benefit of the doubt, but Caleb nodded slightly and took the seat beside me. "Just remember, Cain, I'll hunt you down if you do anything to hurt her - got it?"

"Is this the way you treat all the guys who like Lindsey, or am I just special?"

"I'm not sure yet," he said, clenching his jaw.

"How can you not be sure?"

"Since we moved here, you're the only one she's been interested in. She's been to every one of my games, she's like a best friend to me, and she's way too good for you, so just remember what I said."

"Got it. Duly noted."

The plush, scarlet-colored curtain swished open and all the musicians filed onto the stage, but I was only looking for one in particular. Lindsey wore a long, flowing black dress, her blonde hair pulled to one side with a black ribbon and draped over her shoulder. Her eyes found mine as she walked across the stage, and I might have gasped a little.

"If you say she looks hot, I swear I'll reach down your throat and pull out your lungs," Caleb threatened.

"She's stunning," I said. Although the stage held over a hundred musicians, Lindsey was all I saw.

Classical music wasn't something I was familiar with, and until I'd met Lindsey, I probably would have told you a cello was the Italian word for jello. As ignorant as I was about this kind of music, parts of it were very powerful and emotional. I thought Lindsey was amazing and must have said it out loud, because Caleb whispered something about her being first chair.

After the concert, Lindsey met Caleb and me in front of the theatre. I heard her laughter before I saw her and she was beaming with happiness as she hugged Caleb and thanked him for coming, but Caleb's focus was elsewhere as he looked over Lindsey's shoulder, pointed at his own eyes, then at me. I got the message loud and clear. He'd be watching me.

. . . . . .

When Erin and I had gone out, I'd done about ten percent of the talking, and that's only because she'd ask me questions about how I liked her new purse/shoes/leggings. Whenever I tried to talk about things that interested me, Erin quickly grew bored and steered the conversation back to her. Dinner with Lindsey was completely different.

Lindsey and I talked about soccer, which she understood, since she'd been going to Caleb's games for years, and discovered we had similar tastes in music. Sharing a love of horror movies was just chocolate icing on the cake. Not once did Lindsey mention her wardrobe or what she planned to buy at the mall next week. Talking to her came so naturally, it was almost surreal.

After dinner, I asked Lindsey if she wanted to take a walk around the Battery before we went home. The full moon resembled a golden sphere hovering over the water, and the lofty palm trees swayed in the breeze as we strolled along the sidewalk in front of the stately antebellum homes. The lights of Fort Sumter twinkled in the distance.

"I'm glad I put a change of clothes in the car before the concert. I'd have looked pretty ridiculous strolling the Battery in a long black dress."

"People might have thought you were leading one of those ghost walks. I've seen some of those women in long dresses."

I didn't consider myself a romantic – I wasn't smooth enough for anything like that, but with a beautiful setting like this and the perfect girl by my side, I did get some ideas in my head. Could I really pull this off?

Taking a deep breath, I accidentally/purposely grazed my hand against Lindsey's as she walked beside me, then intertwined our fingers. And she didn't pull away. Instead, she turned and looked up at me, making my stomach flip flop and sending a warm tingling sensation all the way up my arm.

We stopped and I stared down into her blue eyes that seemed to match the color of the evening sky. A gust of wind caught a strand of her hair, blowing it across her face. Catching it in my fingers, I gently tucked it behind her ear, leaned down, and brushed my lips across hers.

CHAPTER 18

"Come back, Cain. I'm right here. Find my voice."

Lindsey. I heard her, but she sounded distant, and maybe slightly panicked? What had happened? The last thing I remembered was getting up enough nerve to kiss her, and now I was almost unconscious? I felt her stroking the hair back from my forehead as she calmly, but urgently tried to wake me.

"Cain, wake up."

I felt so tired and my eyelids seemed to weigh a ton. I struggled to lift them, and through a narrow slit, I saw Lindsey gazing down at me, her brows furrowed in concern.

"There you are. Look at me, Cain."

Not wanting to cause Lindsey any more worry, I obeyed and slowly opened my eyes. From my vantage point, I could see her troubled expression, the palm trees behind her, and the full moon in the star-studded sky. The unyielding surface beneath me was a park bench.

"What happened?"

"You tell me. You left me weak in the knees after tucking my hair behind my ear, gave me an earth shattering kiss, then started to pass out. I managed to get you over to the bench before you went down completely. I've gotten compliments on my kissing, but can't say I've ever affected a guy like that before."

"Earth shattering? Really?" I probably looked like a grinning lunatic loopy on drugs, but I really didn't care.

"That's what you took from what I said? Cain, that wasn't all that happened. When you slumped over, I was afraid I wasn't going to be able to support you, I mean you've got about seventy pounds on me. Then you seemed to wake up, and I was able to steer you in the direction of the bench."

I tried to sit up, but the world started to spin, and I grabbed the back of the bench to steady myself.

"Cain, don't try to get up yet, lie down. Once I got you over here, you started saying things that really confused me. Do you remember?"

"All I remember is the earth shattering kiss, then hearing your voice. What was I saying?"

"You said not to trust him, he's just like all the other guys. Don't believe anything he tells you and get away from him while you still can. You were frantic and tried pushing me away from you. It was kind of scary, Cain, because it's like I was with someone else and it wasn't you talking. What did you mean? Who were you talking about?"

I was positive those words weren't my own. There's no chance in the universe I'd be trying to push Lindsey away from me. Finn's theory was correct. Sarah had been taking over my body whenever she felt like it. And that scared the bejesus out of me. My body wasn't my own and she could be here right now.

"Where's my phone?" I asked, struggling to sit up again.

"I've got it right here, but I don't think you're ready to get up yet, and I can't get you back to the car by myself. Is this related to your concussion? Should I call your mom?"

When I began seeing stars, and not the ones in the sky, I knew Lindsey was right. I wasn't getting off this bench by myself. "No. Please...don't call my Mom, trust me. Call Finn...tell him I need his help," I managed to get out before the darkness fell again.

· · · · ·

"........wrong with him? This isn't normal, Finn. Maybe we should call an ambulance."

The ache in my back told me I hadn't moved from the park bench. How long had I been out this time? Unless Finn had happened to be nearby, it would have taken him at least twenty minutes to drive here, and that didn't count trying to find parking. "Dude, you were right," I mumbled.

"Of course I was. I usually am, but what about this time?"

"Sarah. She was here and took over. She drained my energy and that's why I'm lying here like a wet noodle."

"Sarah? No one named Sarah was here. See, Finn, I told you he was delirious and needs to see a doctor," Lindsey argued.

"Lindsey, Cain and I have something to tell you and you may find it pretty hard to believe, but I promise you, we're not making it up. Right now, we need to get Cain to my car. I'll drive him to my house and tell his mom he's spending the night. You follow us in his car."

"What story? Can you explain what's happening?"

"I promise we'll tell you everything when we get to my house."

· · · · ·

"So what's the verdict? Are you ready to recommend a psych consultation for both of us?" Finn asked.

Finn, Lindsey, and I were in his basement, which was really more a rec/movie room, complete with a floor to ceiling projector screen and plush, sit-in-them-and-never-want-to-leave theatre seats and couches. Being best friends with Finn had its perks.

I felt stronger, which made me believe Sarah had retreated back to the attic. Still unclear on her boundaries, if there were any, Finn had made the decision to come here, not wanting to chance that she would overhear us talking at my house.

"There's the ghost of a missing student living in your attic," Lindsey said, sitting adjacent to me on one of the couches, leaning over with her elbows on her knees and hands clasped together.

"Yes."

"And you're not sure yet what happened to her, but it involved three football players in our class."

"Correct."

"And this ghost, Sarah, has been the cause of your blackouts because she takes over your body and has her own agenda."

"Apparently. Is this too much crazy for you, Lindsey? I'd understand if you just turned around, walked out of here and pretended we'd never met," I said, hoping deep in my gut that wouldn't be her reaction.

And then that high wattage, make-me-forget-my-own-name smile lit up her face. "Now why would I want to walk out on someone who made me weak in the knees when he kissed me earlier?"

With the sudden flush of warmth, I was pretty sure my face matched the color of the red throw pillow beside me, but I didn't care, as long as Lindsey wasn't leaving.

Finn swiveled toward me, his mouth hanging open in shock. "Wait, did you hear that?" he asked, hand to his ear. "Listen – do you hear it?"

"What are you talking about? I don't hear anything."

"Yep. I was right. It's the sound of women from all over swooning at the thought of kissing you." And then he laughed so hard he snorted. How he ever got women to go out with him was a mystery.

"Finn, you're an ass," Lindsey said, rolling her eyes. That might have been the first time it wasn't me saying it. "Actually, Cain, I think I can help you."

"Seriously? How?"

"So, you're a medium, or one of those people who helps ghosts cross over? Can you exorcise Cain?" Finn asked.

"No, Finn, I'm not a medium and of course I can't exorcise spirits, but I do believe in ghosts. I guess you could say I've practically been surrounded by them my whole life. Have I ever told you about my Aunt Mona?"

Both of us shook our heads. Other than Caleb, I didn't know much about Lindsey's family, but if Aunt Mona could help us, I might consider kissing her senseless, too. Then again, maybe I should wait and see what she looked like first.

"Is she a Ghostbuster?"

"Finn, can you please refrain and listen?" I asked, holding up my hand in his direction. "Lindsey, how can your aunt help us?"

"She has this really....unique place on King Street. She owns a kind of metaphysical store and sells crystals, herbs, incense, tarot cards – stuff like that. I could spend hours just browsing, and the books she has – it's a fascinating place."

I moved my hand to her knee and squeezed it gently. "It sounds really cool, but how can any of that help with keeping Sarah away from me?"

"Aunt Mona also sells amulets and talismans. They have different purposes, but can help protect you from things or increase the energy in different areas of your life. She can explain it better, but it couldn't hurt to see her."

The shop sounded like a good place to begin. It's not like Finn and I were covered up with an avalanche of ideas. "Is she a medium or psychic?"

"Well, let's just say she's always been able to sense things about people and places. She doesn't advertise it, but I know that over the years people have come to her for help, some wanting to get rid of spirits, others wanting to make contact. She's not one hundred percent successful, but she's always willing to try.

"Mom said she was always like that, even when they were young. Knowing who was on the phone before it was answered, having dreams about things before they happened. She even described my dad and told mom she'd marry him before they'd even met."

"Uh, yeah – we need to talk to her. If she can't help me, maybe she knows someone who can. When can we meet her?"

"She's out of town, but will be back in a couple of days. I'll call and give her the details and see when she can meet with us."

"Okay, so we've got a game plan now. Good to know. How about we discuss the sleeping arrangements for tonight?" Finn asked, waggling his eyebrows.

Lindsey stood and teasingly punched Finn in the shoulder. "My sleeping arrangements include me sleeping by myself in my own bed in my own room."

Finn huffed heavily. "You're no fun, Lindsey. Did anyone ever tell you that?"

CHAPTER 19

Sarah was waiting for me after school the next day. In a daze, I walked into my bedroom, thinking about the kiss with Lindsey after the concert, and nearly jumped out of my skin when I saw Sarah sitting on my bed, arms crossed over her chest, glaring at me, her face twisted into a menacing expression.

"Don't you want to know what happened to me?" she spat. Compared to the last time I'd seen her, Sarah's features were disturbingly solid, and not very ghostly at all. Except for those empty, soulless black eyes.

Any other time I found something otherworldly waiting for me with a look like that, I'd be cowering. Not this time. My anger overrode the fear. "Maybe later," I said, throwing my backpack on the desk. "What I'd really like to know is where you get off high-jacking my body?"

Sarah raised her barely-there eyebrows in surprise. "So, you finally figured it out. After your head injury, your body's natural defenses were compromised and left you wide open, so I just slipped in. It was too tempting of an opportunity to pass up."

Just. Slipped. In. "You have no right to take over my body! What makes you think it's okay to do that to someone?" My hands were clenching and unclenching at my sides. "Finn and I wanted to help you, but you've crossed a boundary – you're miles over it. How can you expect us to trust you now?"

Sarah lunged at me, but outrage fueled my courage and I stood my ground this time. She stopped a few inches away and although a good six or seven inches shorter, she hovered so that we were eye level with each other. If I'd stopped to consider that a ghost was literally in my face threatening me, I'd probably rethink my decision to stay here, but in some way, I felt as if this was a test. If I backed down now, there's no telling what else Sarah might do.

"*I* say it's alright! The loss of my life gives me the right to do whatever I want! I was just a bet between the three of them so they could see who I'd choose to sleep with once they got a few drinks in me. I was *nothing* to them."

Sarah's anger and hurt seethed out of her with an intensity that made them almost tangible. She'd wanted to believe that for the first time in her life, someone liked her for who she was, not because of what they could get from her. I'd seen the types of girls those three guys hung with, and they were nothing like Sarah. Even though she'd committed the ultimate invasion of privacy when she'd leaped into my body, I could understand her feelings. But that still didn't make it alright. "Look, I'm sorry for what happened to you, I really am, but using me to spy on them, or whatever else you're planning to do isn't an option! Do you get that?"

Her unwavering gaze never left mine, but I could feel her withdraw a little, reigning in the fury. "Yes, Cain, I *get* it," she sneered.

I felt my muscles unclench slightly, relieved to see she'd backed off somewhat. "I'm serious, Sarah, no more, or you're on your own." Backing away, I sat in the desk chair, fixated on her. My gut was telling me not to relax just yet. "Now, do you want to tell me the rest of the story?"

Sarah lowered herself so that her feet touched the floor. She studied my face, as if trying to determine whether I was sincere and if she should continue to trust me. Imagine that. After I'd experienced the whole invasion of the body snatchers ordeal, she was questioning *my* trustworthiness. Whatever she'd seen must have reassured her, because she continued.

"So you were a bet between them? What do you mean?"

"Liam and Nathan bet Jacob he couldn't get me to go out with him. But I did, and once I figured out the real reason they'd asked me here, the stakes changed and I tried to leave. I just wanted to go home."

"But you didn't make it home. What happened?"

Sarah moved to the window overlooking the street while she spoke, tilting her head back and closing her eyes, like she enjoyed the sun shining on her face. "When they realized I was leaving, they tried to convince me to stay. I refused, so they decided to physically restrain me. I screamed and fought, but it was three big guys against one of me. We scuffled, there was pushing and pulling, and I fell, hitting my head on one of the boards lying on the floor. I was hurt, but knew what would happen if I didn't leave. When I tried to run again, the room was spinning and blood was running down my forehead into my eyes. I took off the scarf I was wearing and used it to wipe off the blood, then tied it around my head. The blood scared them, and they backed off when I staggered across the floor toward the stairs. I just wanted to get out of there and go home, pretend the whole thing never happened."

She seemed detached, like she was reading the story from a book or talking about someone else. "But then I felt someone push me down the attic stairs. The end. My life was over because of an idiotic bet between three guys who went on with their lives like nothing happened. I never got to accept that scholarship and go to college. I never had a boyfriend. I never got to see what I could be on my own, away from my parents and all their restrictions, and I'll never have the opportunity to spend my life with someone and grow old together."

The air of detachment vanished as she turned to face me, her anger rushing to the surface again. "So when I had the chance to stow away in your body and watch them, to find out if they had turned themselves in, or were at least suffering and feeling guilty, I took it. You're damn right I took it."

Her callous, piercing black eyes sparkled with rage and I felt the negative energy swirling around me. It wasn't a good feeling – as if Sarah was leeching the life force from my body and replacing it with darkness and emptiness.

"I've never hurt you, Sarah, and I don't owe you anything, but I'll say it again. You cannot use me like a Trojan horse to spy on Jacob, Liam, and Nathan. I get why you feel cheated - who wouldn't? You lost everything. Finn and I want to help you, but you're making that pretty difficult, so do something like that again and you're out of my house."

Sarah continued her stone cold glare and my body was poised to run, but I was afraid if I turned my back on her, she'd attack like some wild animal and take me down.

"I already told you, Cain. I get it," she hissed. "I'll stay out of your body."

The tension I'd been holding in my shoulders began to melt away. "Great. Awesome. Now, can you give me anything, some kind of proof we could take to the police? Did anyone know you were here with them that night?"

"No one knew. I had no close friends and my parents thought I was somewhere else. They didn't allow me to date, not that anyone had ever asked, and never would have let me go if I'd told them the truth." Sarah now sat on the bed like statue, unmoving. When she wasn't on the verge of a maelstrom of destruction, she was perfectly still, with no human gestures like touching her face or hair, shifting around. It was unnerving.

"I know the police found traces of your blood here, but the newspaper said there were no leads. Do you think Jacob, Nathan, or Liam told anyone?"

"Who knows? Even if they'd told someone, it looks like no one came forward with any information, so they're probably keeping the secret for them, and there's no way they'd turn on each other."

She was right about that. It had been several months since her death and the three of them were still tight, so it was doubtful that would change. I had another question for Sarah, but was hesitant to ask, afraid of her reaction. My body could wind up splattered against the wall, in the yard two stories down, or in pieces scattered about the house. But it had to be asked.

"Um, Sarah, there's something else that might help," I said, rubbing the back of my neck, my gaze focused on the floor. Reluctantly, I raised my head. "Do you know where your body is?"

The room had been cold before, but it felt as if the temperature plummeted in the span of a heartbeat, making it a distinct possibility I could be flash frozen. Sarah was immobile, absolutely no movement. Behind her eyes, I could see something going on, but they remained glittering steel orbs, giving nothing away.

"No. I have no idea," she answered in a flat voice.

"Can't you maybe sense where it might be? Some kind of connection? A strong feeling?"

"No. There's nothing." And then Sarah was gone.

The temperature of the room began to climb and I could breathe freely again. I was relieved she'd left, but felt something heavy in the air, the weight of it on my shoulders. Sarah had lied to me. I was almost positive she knew the location of her body.

CHAPTER 20

"So, not only is she a body-snatching, man-hating ghost with breathtaking anger management issues, she's also a compulsive liar? Do you think there are support groups for ghosts? Is that a thing?"

After having Finn as my best friend for over ten years, you'd think I'd know how his mind worked and nothing that fell out of his mouth would surprise me. But you'd be wrong. He was completely unpredictable at times, but I could always count on him for an honest answer or opinion. Freakish and out of left field occasionally, but honest. And highly entertaining. "So, you're suggesting we get Sarah into therapy? Maybe having an intervention?"

"Seems like it would make her afterlife a little more pleasant, don't you think? I mean, we're talking a long period of time here, right? Maybe if she interacted with more ghosts, she'd learn to fit in better, make some friends. Stop living in your body. Just saying."

"If you're finished, I need to ask you something. Should we talk to Jacob, Nathan, and Liam? Tell them she's still here and what she's saying?"

Finn sat back heavily in his cafeteria chair and blinked once, slowly. "There are so many reasons not to do that, I don't even know where to begin."

"Why?" I asked, pushing away my tray that held a half-eaten cheeseburger. "I just feel like maybe we should warn them. Sarah seems on the verge of something, but I'm not sure what. She's oozing anger from every pore and that can't be a good thing."

"So let me get this straight. You'd go up to them and say, 'Hey, guys, I hear you tried to lure Sarah Butler into a house under construction, get her drunk, then rape her, but the whole plan went sideways, and you wound up killing her. Sarah's ghost told us this herself. And by the way, can you tell us where you put the body?' Do you think they'd laugh first or just commence with the beatings?

"Seriously, Cain, if they find out we know anything, and that's assuming they believed us, they'd try to stop us from turning them in. If we even had proof. We can't walk into a police station and tell them we know what happened to Sarah Butler because her ghost is living in your attic."

Well - there was that. They'd probably jump me first, then stand back and laugh about it. But they had to be held accountable for what they'd done. "What should we do? Lindsey's aunt won't be back in town until tomorrow, but I hate just sitting around, waiting for Sarah to do something else."

Finn shot a glance over his shoulder, at the table where Jacob, Nathan, and Liam were sitting and laughing with their friends. "If Sarah is really lying about knowing where her body is, and I don't know why she'd do that, but if she is, maybe she's also lying about how everything went down. If the four of them were struggling, especially at the top of the attic stairs, who says she was even pushed? Seems like it would have been easy for her to lose her balance, or trip and fall down the stairs on her own."

Finn had a good point. As much as I despised those three for what they'd done to Sarah, if that was truly what had happened, it might have been an accident and Sarah was either confused or looking for someone to blame. "How could we even find out if she's telling the truth?"

Finn gulped down half a bottle of water before answering, then wiped his mouth with the back of his hand. "I'm not sure yet, but if those guys are guilty, yeah, they should pay, justice served, and all that. But unless Sarah's body is found, there's no new evidence because no one's going to believe her ghost is living in your attic. I think what we need to be concerned about right now is meeting Lindsey's aunt and seeing if she can A, keep you from being Sarah's plaything, and 2, send her to the light, her grave, or wherever she should have gone in the first place."

"You're getting your 1's and 2's and A's and B's mixed up again. Anyway, and try not to let this go to your head, but you're right. We don't have any proof right now. If we figure out where her body is, maybe the police can find more evidence, something that could prove those three are responsible."

"Ah, my young Padawan, when will you learn to place your trust in Finn, who is all-knowing and all-seeing."

"If you were all-knowing and all-seeing, I wouldn't be in this mess right now."

. . . . .

Since Sarah had been making her nocturnal visits, I'd become a light sleeper, which also explained why I felt exhausted much of the time. When the attic door creaked open that night, I immediately heard it.

"Come on, Sarah," I said, pulling a pillow over my head, "I need some sleep tonight. We can talk tomorrow, alright?"

No response. I knew she was here because of the drop in room temperature, but I felt Eby tensed up at my side, surprised he hadn't dashed out of here. I let out a huff, rolled over and sat up, figuring she was going to do what she wanted anyway, and sleep would have to wait. She was standing at the foot of my bed, light from the street lamp creating an aura around her. But something was different.

Watching various nature shows over the years, I knew some animals sensed when a predator was near, their self-preservation instincts the strongest they possessed. That's exactly how I felt right now. I was the prey. Sarah looked nothing like the innocent, victimized, shy high school girl she liked to portray. She was the embodiment of evil, her black eyes reflective pools of malevolence, hands stretching towards me as if reaching for my throat.

As she cocked her head very slightly to her left, a confident, victorious leer stretched across her face. Everything inside me said to run, but I couldn't get to the door without going by her and knew I'd never make it.

With my hand on Eby's back, I felt a rumble go through him as he growled at Sarah. Crouched on all fours, his body was rigid and I figured he was as nervous about running by her as I was. Sarah slowly rose off the floor, and I felt the muscles in Eby's haunches grow even tauter in anticipation.

What happened next was over in the blink of an eye, but I saw everything as if in slow motion. Sarah shot toward me like a bullet out of a gun. Simultaneously, Eby leaped in front of me, attempting to block Sarah from reaching me. Although a valiant effort, Eby had no effect on Sarah and sailed right through her semi-transparent shape, but I loved my brave furry friend for trying.

When she hit my chest, I felt it at my core, like a wrecking ball had plowed into me. But she didn't just hit me, Sarah was inside me again and I could feel her moving, as I felt myself fading, my life energy being drained. When Sarah had been a passenger within me before, I'd never felt her presence. This feeling was completely foreign to me. She was something palpable, not like an internal organ, but more of an extension of myself, an extra arm or leg. Just before my world went black, I had a brief connection with Sarah's corrupted mind and the atrocities I saw made me welcome the darkness as it enveloped me.

CHAPTER 21

"Wakey wakey, sleeping beauty. If you think I'm kissing you first, think again, Cain."

"Finn, did it occur to you maybe he wants me to kiss him and not you? Get out of the way and let the princess rescue the prince for a change."

Lindsey's soft lips pressed against mine and if this was a dream, I didn't want to wake up. Maybe if I pretended to be asleep she'd keep kissing me. It was worth a try.

"Seriously, Cain, I know it's Saturday, but you've gotta wake up. There're some massively important things to discuss and then we need to get over to Aunt Mona's at hyper speed. Quit with the kissing and slap him, Lindsey. I know my boy and I guarantee he's awake and just hoping you'll keep kissing him if he stays quiet."

How did he know? Finn should have invoked the guy code rule number 8, section B3 that said if a friend was otherwise engaged in kissing and/or related activities, said activities couldn't be interrupted unless blood or death were involved.

"I know what you're thinking, Cain, and I have grounds for interruption. Death is involved."

What? My eyes snapped open as Lindsey's warm lips left mine, focusing first on her, sitting on the bed gazing down at me, then Finn, standing behind Lindsey, a serious expression on his face. Stern, even. An entirely foreign appearance for Finn.

As I tried to sit up, I realized my arms wouldn't move. Or my legs. Could I talk? "I can't move." I guess I could. So, everything above the shoulders seemed to be in working order, but everything below was motionless. My extremities strained to shift even an inch, but they might as well have been dead weights attached to my body.

"Seriously, Cain, it's one in the afternoon. Are you that lazy? "

"Shut up, Finn. Look at his face – something's wrong. Cain, what happened?"

Then the horrors of last night came rushing back. Sarah's malevolent smile, the overwhelming feeling of danger, Eby's act of bravery, and the feeling of Sarah invading my body. Eby. My heart sank. Was he alright?

"Eby. Did you see him when you came in?" I asked, my stomach rolling in the fear that Sarah had hurt him.

"Eby did this to you? I always knew that cat was hiding something and up to no good."

"Finn, were you raised by wild hogs? Eby was downstairs on the screened porch sleeping in the sun. He's fine, Cain," Lindsey reassured me, gripping my hand.

"It was her. Sarah." Then I relayed the grisly details of last night.

"Cain, you must have been petrified! And Eby – he tried to protect you."

"I've always felt weak after Sarah 'borrowed' me, but never like this. Never incapacitated," I said, still trying to wiggle my fingers, toes, anything.

"It's like she literally sucked your energy right out of you," Finn said, his brow furrowing. "And after that, you were here all night, right?"

"Look at me, Finn. I can't even lift my arms. How would I go anywhere when I can't get out of bed?"

Finn and Lindsey looked at each other, silently communicating something I wasn't privy to. "I guess him being like this could account for what happened, if you believe in that sort of thing, right?"

Lindsey nodded. "My aunt can probably explain it better, but the chances of it being a coincidence are pretty astronomical."

Now I was just annoyed. Besides lying in bed like a useless lump of Play-Doh, the two of them acted as if I wasn't even here. "Would someone tell what's going on? Finn, you said it involved death. What happened?"

"Liam Brooks is dead."

What? I blinked slowly. A unicorn bursting through my door with Thor on its back wouldn't have surprised me more. "He's......dead?" Lindsey ran her hand across my shoulder and up through my hair. "How?" I was afraid to hear, but needed to know the answer.

"It was a car accident. Kind of," Finn added. "He ran off the road."

"And this happened last night?"

"Yeah. He'd been with Jacob and Nathan, but dropped them off and was driving home. They last saw him around eleven o'clock last night and he was found early this morning. Do you think Sarah had something to do with his death?"

Was it possible Sarah had killed Liam? Could ghosts do that? A week ago, I wasn't even sure I believed in ghosts. Now I had proof of their existence, so what made me think Sarah wasn't capable of murder? With all the rage and anger she'd been holding onto, she would definitely hurt the three of them if given the opportunity. But murder? Then I remembered how Sarah had looked last night, the way my instincts told me in no uncertain terms that I was in danger.

"I don't know, but driving off the side of the road late at night and hitting something isn't uncommon. Why do you think she might be responsible?"

"Did I say he hit anything?" Liam was dead, but didn't hit anything? Maybe the car rolled?

"You know my dad's a journalist, right, Cain?" I nodded. Lindsey had mentioned it at dinner the other night, but I'd almost forgotten about her dad working for the local newspaper. "This information doesn't leave the room, because it could cause trouble for him. I heard him on the phone this morning. Liam ran off the road, but the car was found in a grassy area, still running, headlights on. He hadn't hit anything, and there was no damage to the car.

"The thing is, Liam's head was nearly torn from his body. No windows were broken, so it wasn't from the glass, no weapons were found, and there were no traces of footprints around the car. I can't imagine what he went through. What a horrible way to die." Lindsey's eyes were rimmed with tears. If my arms had worked, they'd be around her right now.

"With you being all useless like this, I guess Sarah was able to absorb enough energy to get out of here, hunt down Liam, and kill him. I can't believe I just said that about a ghost. Are we on *Supernatural*? Did I miss something?"

Then it hit me. And just the possibility that it could have happened was enough to steal the breath from my body and clench my soul. "You were asking if I'd been here all night because you thought Sarah might have used me to kill Liam."

"Well, yeah." Finn replied.

"No," Lindsey said firmly, challenging Finn to disagree with her. But he did, of course.

"Look, Cain, I know there's not a chance in the world you'd have hurt Liam. But you weren't you last night and when Sarah was in control before, you didn't always know where you'd been or what you'd done."

I gritted my teeth. "I didn't kill Liam." Finn searched my face for any hint of doubt in my involvement, but finding none, he nodded once.

"We know you didn't. You couldn't. But the sooner we get to my aunt's place, the better. How are you feeling now, Cain?"

Testing the waters again, I discovered my limbs were moving slightly. Nowhere near the full range of motion, but it was better than nothing. "I'm starving. Maybe if I eat something, it would help."

Lindsey grinned, then kissed my cheek. "I'll go downstairs and fix you a sandwich. Finn, make yourself useful and get him in the shower while I'm gone," she said, slapping him on the back as she headed out the door.

Finn eyes widened. "What? That's just all kinds of wrong. I know how to make sandwiches! Why don't you get him in the shower?"

"Finn, we've showered in the same locker room for years. It's nothing you haven't seen before," I said, struggling to sit up.

"But this is different. It's only us and it's so…..up close and personal."

"Just get in the bathroom, start the shower, then close your eyes."

. . . . .

A hot shower and food worked miracles in restoring my energy, and I was walking almost normally by the time we got to King Street. Aunt Mona's shop wasn't too far from Market Street, and considering how often Mom had dragged me to the open air markets there, I was surprised I'd never noticed it before. Walking into Mystical Magic was like being transported to another world. And it was a really good-smelling world full of colorful crystals, unusual jewelry, old books, loose leaf teas, and a wide assortment of things I couldn't identify.

It looked as if the original wood floors were intact, with exposed brick and built-in bookshelves, giving it that old Charleston charm. Some of the free-standing shelves looked like they were made of reclaimed wood and the arched doorways matched the era of the building. Not that I sat around watching HGTV with Mom, but with her being a realtor, I'd picked up on a lot of industry lingo and details. And it was kind of cool, preserving a bit of history instead of opening a store in a strip mall that lacked the warmth and personality of Mystical Magic

The music playing in the background was that calming stuff, like what Mom played when she practiced yoga. Overall, the place had a very serene and welcoming vibe.

"It smells better in here than new leather soccer shoes. Almost," Finn said.

"It's yellow sandalwood, an aid in seeking peace and calmness," a throaty voice said from behind me, causing me to stiffen in surprise.

I turned to see Lindsey standing with a woman who could almost be Lindsey herself in thirty years. They were nearly identical in facial features, eye color, and build, but where Lindsey's hair was blond and wavy, this woman had long coils of copper ringlets, although they may have been outnumbered by the bracelets along both her arms. Mona made a distinct clinking sound when she moved.

Lindsey had one arm looped through Mona's. "This is Finn and Cain. Guys, my Aunt Mona."

"It's so nice to meet friends of my favorite niece," Mona said, using her other arm to shake Finn's hand.

"Your only niece," Lindsey laughed, leaning in to kiss Mona's cheek.

As Mona shifted to me and the warmth of her hand enveloped mine, she froze, scrutinizing my face. "Oh, it's you alright." My eyebrows puckered in confusion.

Lindsey placed her arm around Mona's shoulder and gently pulled her away, while she still observed me. "I didn't give her any details about what's been going on, just that one of you is having troubles and needs some help."

"How can you tell it's me just by touching my hand?"

"Honey, I felt it the second you walked through the door, before I even saw you. Negative energy is wrapped around you like a blanket. I can feel that whatever it is, it almost drained you recently and you're barely standing right now. How about we go back to my office and talk."

Without waiting for an answer, Mona looked over her shoulder and spoke to a younger woman at the register. "Claire, I'll be in my office if you need anything." Putting one arm around my back and draping the other over Lindsey's shoulder, Mona guided us to the back of the store. "Once I hear what you have to say, Cain, we'll come up with some things to help you, although I have a couple of ideas already."

"Any kind of help sounds really good right about now," I said, grateful Mona was willing to try. The twinge building in my chest just might be a tiny spark of hope.

Chapter 22

After Finn, Lindsey, and I finished relaying the sordid tale of Sarah, Mona sat immobile behind her desk, hands clasped, staring down. Several towers of books and jars of unidentified substances cluttered her desk and the shelves around the office and I was afraid any sudden movements could be disastrous.

Mona pushed her squeaky chair away from the desk and slowly stood, then wandered over to a window and observed the pedestrians ambling by on the sidewalk. Finn mouthed "What's wrong with her?" to Lindsey, who shrugged her shoulders in reply, then slid her hand into mine. I never realized how comforting it could be to hold someone's hand. Erin's pink talons used to pull and claw at me, tugging me here or there, usually someplace I had no interest in going. Lindsey's hand was soft and warm and fit perfectly in my own. Guess it just had to be the right person.

While I studied our intertwined hands, Mona cleared her throat, then turned to face us. "Okay, here's what I'm thinking based on what you've told me and what I see and feel in Cain. Clearly, Sarah was wronged in some way, but we're not positive she was murdered by those boys. Still, she feels cheated at the loss of her life and is separated from her loved ones, so we have a vengeful spirit seeking retribution.

"Cain, after your concussion, your body and mind's ability to guard itself was weakened and Sarah realized she could take advantage of this, becoming a passenger which enabled her to see what was happening in the lives of the boys she feels are responsible for her death. Sarah saw them going about their lives, showing no remorse, and doing things she'll never have the opportunity to experience. It's like she never mattered.

"I'm sure you understand by now that your blackouts occurred when Sarah drew on your strength and essentially took over your body, expressing what she really thought about Erin and her distrust of men in general to

Lindsey. You were drawn to the football field because Sarah was watching them."

I shifted in my chair, still uncomfortable knowing that Sarah had been in the driver's seat. "We figured that was probably the deal. What I don't understand exactly is what happened to me last night? Liam is dead. I know I didn't kill him, but how could Sarah be responsible? She's a ghost and they can't really hurt people, right? I mean, knocking a person around a little, wreaking some havoc in the house every now and then, but murder?"

Mona walked around the desk and knelt in front of me, placing her hands on my knees. "Cain, honey, I wish I could tell you that you're right, but I can't. It's true, most ghosts are harmless. Maybe they're here because they don't realize they're dead, or they choose to stay in a place where they were happiest during their life. Sometimes they have unfinished business they hope to take care of and some ghosts want to stay close to their loved ones and watch over them."

"I don't think any of those things fit into Sarah's agenda," Finn said.

Mona stood, sighing heavily. "Unfortunately, you're right, Finn. Sarah's animosity toward the boys, her outrage over what was done to her, and even her own self-loathing for allowing herself to be tricked has been brewing for all these months. Finding out that the boys not only got away with what they did, but show no remorse and have gone on with their lives has fueled her, making her stronger and more desperate for revenge.

"Last night, Sarah managed to discover a way to absorb most of Cain's life energy, giving her enough strength to move about freely without the need of his body. Her anger is escalating and I'm certain she won't stop at killing only one of the boys."

I didn't like the way this was sounding at all. Things were bad - I mean, Liam had been murdered in a tragic, unspeakable way and according to Mona, Sarah had only just begun Operation Revenge. "Are you saying she'll try to siphon off more energy from me? I had no way of defending myself last night."

Mona leaned against the edge of her desk, crossing her arms over her chest. "Do you want the good news or the bad news first?"

"Um....good, I think. I could really use something good right about now," I said, my voice wavering slightly.

"Okay. I don't think Sarah needs to draw any more energy from you, Cain. She took enough last night to sustain her for a while. The bad news is that the act of killing only makes her more powerful. She absorbed whatever Liam had to give and the longer Sarah remains in this realm, the stronger she'll become, especially since she knows the other two boys are still alive and well."

"Wait," Finn interrupted, "You mean she grows stronger the longer she's around?"

"In this case, it's highly likely. When a person's life is taken, especially if it's very suddenly, their spirit may not even realize they've passed on at first, so they're confused and unsure of what happened or where to go. The longer they remain in this plane, the angrier they become, especially, as in Sarah's case, when they understand what has happened to them and hope to gain justice against the people responsible for their death. Sarah has been here for several months now, and even in the short time since she latched onto Cain, look how forceful she's become."

From hanging out in my attic and scaring Eby, writing in condensation on the bathroom mirror, and opening and closing the attic door, to murder? Yeah, Sarah was far more powerful and thinking that she might be waiting for me when I got home gave me a sinking, heavy feeling in the pit of my stomach.

"So, what should we do now? Do you think Sarah will just leave my house?"

Mona tilted her head, raised her bracelet-clad arm and placed her hand on my shoulder. "Oh, Cain, I really wish it was that simple, honey."

Somehow I knew that would be too easy. Sarah also didn't strike me as someone whose persistence wavered.

"Is there anything we can do, Aunt Mona? Is there some way we can keep her from hurting Cain or anyone else again?" Lindsey asked, voicing my own thoughts.

Mona went over toward the cluttered shelves, shuffling jars and boxes, searching for something. "I have a couple of ideas, some things that can help you right now, honey. Now where did I put...."

As Mona mumbled to herself while she combed through her shelves, I squeezed Lindsey's hand. "Thanks for bringing me here, Lindsey. If I hadn't met Mona, I don't know what I'd do."

"If we hadn't gotten you out of the house this afternoon, Sarah might have strung you up and beat you like a piñata to amuse herself between killings," Finn said, ever the brutally honest friend. "So yeah, you're welcome."

"Finn, how can you even joke about something like that?" Lindsey admonished.

"It's called a diversion tactic, sweetheart. If I didn't do something, Cain would do nothing but worry and withdraw into himself. He'd become a basket case instead of work on a solution to the problem."

"And how do you know he'd become a basket case? Considering everything he's been through, I think he's handling it pretty well."

"I saw it after his dad's accident and I won't let it happen to him again," Finn said, his tone rigid.

Lindsey's eyes glistened, she nodded once, and lowered her head.

After my Dad died, all I'd thought about was Mom and Maddie and what would happen to my family without him. Finn had stayed with me, listening to my ramblings, offering suggestions, helping with Maddie, or just sitting quietly, letting me know he was there. He'd pulled me into activities – soccer, movies, video games – anything to give my mind a break. I don't know what would have happened if he hadn't been there for me.

The sound of Mona's bracelets clacking together brought our attention back to her. If she had something to help me, I'd give her every bit of my attention.

"I finally found what I was looking for. I keep telling myself I'll clean out this office someday, but that day never seems to come around. Now, Cain, to start off, I want you to wear this amulet."

Mona held out a silver medallion on a long, black leather cord. It was about 1.5 inches in diameter, with a black background, and several silver circles surrounding four small stars of David. Dangling in front of me, it caught the late afternoon sunlight, the glint from the silver momentarily blinding me.

"This is called The Magic Circle of Solomon. Wear it at all times to protect you from evil spirits. Don't even take if off when you shower or sleep." I nodded as Mona placed it over my head, the amulet settling just above the level of my heart, then she swung back to her desk to pick up ..... twigs of grass tied together?

"Would this be for medicinal purposes or can anyone have some?" Finn asked.

Lindsey's eyes shot lasers at Finn as she shook her head. Mona made an unsuccessful attempt to hide her laughter.

"This is a smudge stick made of mountain sage, sweetgrass, and cedar. Light this and let it burn while you walk through your house, spending more time in the areas where Sarah lingers. This will help with purification and banishment. Remember, Cain, these are not permanent solutions, but may aid in keeping Sarah a safe distance from you."

I released Lindsey's hand and rubbed my face. Although unconscious for nearly twelve hours, I'd never felt so tired in my life. "Is there anything we can do? Something to get rid of her permanently?"

Mona sighed heavily. "Yes, there's something that will most likely work and is only used in the most dangerous situations. In your case, it would be very difficult, and maybe impossible."

The corner of Finn's mouth quirked up - he always loved a good challenge. "Name it. We'll figure it out somehow," he said.

"In order to remove Sarah from this plane, you need to find her grave, salt her remains, and burn them. This series of actions will cause her to move on."

Lindsey gasped. "But that would mean asking Jacob and Nathan where they buried her..."

"....and getting them to confess to what happened." I finished.

"Well, that sucks," Finn added.

"Exactly," Mona said.

CHAPTER 23

"How are we going to get Jacob and Nathan to tell us where the body is and incriminate themselves? They'll never believe us if we tell them about Sarah," Lindsey said, chewing her lip.

After leaving Mona's, we'd stopped at Jake's Shrimp Shack for takeout, then driven back to Finn's in hopes of formulating a successful game plan. Which was next to impossible. Why would two teenagers readily confess to murdering someone?

We'd looked online for updates on Liam's death. The police had confirmed he'd been murdered, but had no leads so far. They were asking people to come forward if they had any information regarding his death.

"Okay, let's try thinking about this logically," Finn said, right before shoveling golden brown fried shrimp into his mouth.

I nodded, stretching out in my chair, hands clasped behind my head. "If you have any ideas, I'd love to hear them."

"Put yourself in their places right after Sarah fell down the stairs. You lured a girl out to a house under construction by lying to her and were possibly planning to rape her, or at least get her drunk and see where it led. When you realized she wasn't buying into that, you panicked and tried to keep her from leaving. After scuffling, she either fell or was pushed down the stairs, and now you have a body. Calling the police isn't an option, because you're probably responsible for her journey down the stairs. You can't leave her there - she might be traced back to you if her body is found.

"Putting her in the trunk of the car and taking her body somewhere else is too big of a risk. You're already at a construction site where dirt has been moved around and displaced and there's a wooded area behind it. Who's going to notice some more churned up dirt?"

I'd like to say none of this had previously occurred to be me due to lack of sleep and temporary loss of control of my brain and body, but that wasn't entirely the truth. I'd never really thought about it. Of course Sarah was buried around my house somewhere. They couldn't have taken her body very far. The massive basket of fried shrimp and greasy fries I'd consumed wasn't sitting so well now.

"Have you noticed something around your house that could be a grave, Cain?" Lindsey asked.

"Well, I can't say looking for shallow graves in my backyard has been at the top of my to-do list. Then again, maybe I've walked right by it every day and never noticed."

Finn collected empty to-go boxes to throw away, tossing them in the trash can in the corner. "Maybe we should try and find her body ourselves first. Then we could avoid that whole awkward conversation with Jacob and Nathan of where they hid it."

Lindsey knitted her brows. "But Sarah is probably coming after them next. Maybe even while we're sitting here. Don't you think we should warn them?"

Finn barked out a laugh as he flopped back on the couch. "How do you imagine that conversation going, Lindsey? 'Hey, Jacob. The vindictive spirit of the girl you might have killed has returned and just embarked on The Reprisal Tour. You're one of her guaranteed stops, but you probably won't live long enough to tell anyone about it. Thought you'd like to know. Oh, and by the way…where did you put her body? We need to dig her up, salt the remains, and then torch them to get rid of her.' Does that sound about right?"

"You left out the part where he beats the crap out of us."

"I was going with the assumption that his beating the crap out of us was a given. Sorry, Cain. How did you see the conversation going, Princess?"

Lindsey's mouth was set in a hard line. This wasn't going to be pretty. "Maybe I'd handle things a little differently. Something like, 'Jacob, you may want to tell me to get away from you or have me locked up, but what I'm about to say could save your life. I don't know exactly what happened with you and Sarah Butler and I'm not accusing you of anything, but her spirit is still here and she's out for vengeance.

"As proof, I know details of what happened the night she died. She was responsible for Liam's death and you or Nathan are probably next. We want to help you and to do that, we need to know where Sarah's remains are before she hurts someone else.' It sounds a little better coming from someone who has a touch more sensitivity than a brick. Does that sound about right,

Sunshine?"

This needed to be stopped before the two of them threw down in the middle of the floor. "In the interest of dodging a confrontation with Jacob and Nathan and preventing my best friend and girlfriend from killing each other, leaving me to handle everything on my own, how about we search for the grave on our own tomorrow and then go from there? Right now, I need to get home and burn the grass twigs Mona gave me."

Finn clenched his jaw and gave a barely perceptible nod, although his expression was one of admiration. Finn also enjoyed worthy opponents.

"Of course," Lindsey said, her hand finding its way into mine. It was then I realized I'd just called her my girlfriend. Maybe I should have asked her first, but the way she was beaming told me she didn't disagree.

. . . . .

Mom had taken Maddie to a movie, so Finn and I had the house to ourselves, with no one bothering us and asking questions while we 'smudged'. Strange word, but I didn't care what it was called as long as it worked. I'd planned on doing this by myself, but after my experience with Sarah last night, Finn and Lindsey didn't want me to be alone. Although I'd love nothing more than to have Lindsey come over and help me smudge, then spend the night, I didn't think that would fly with Mom. So I was stuck with Finn. Not that I was complaining. The thought of being alone in the house with Sarah sent shivers up my spine.

"I hope we don't run into Sarah while we're doing this," I whispered.

"Yeah, wouldn't that be embarrassing. Or life-threatening. Why are you whispering?"

Finn had a point. Why was I whispering? Like Sarah wouldn't know if we were in the house anyway? "I don't know why I'm whispering, but if we ran into her, I guess we'd know for sure if the protection amulet worked, right?"

Mona had said to start smudging where Sarah spent the most time, so we began in the attic. Once the twig bundle was lit, it gave off a nice, woodsy aroma. Since its purpose was to drive spirits away, I'd expected something more – offensive, I guess, closer to sulfur and brimstone. But considering the potential final destination of Sarah's soul, she might have felt more at home with that smell and less likely to exit the building.

We trudged slowly around the attic, lingering in the corner where Sarah's blood was found, then made our way down the stairs to my bedroom without any sign of her. Maybe the smudging thing worked instantly. Wouldn't that be sweet. The new smell in the house grabbed Eby's attention and he and his inquiring mind trailed us through each room.

"So Eby tried to protect you last night?"

"He tried. He usually speeds out of here at Mach 10, you've seen him, but this time he tried to attack Sarah. I haven't decided if he was courageous or stupid," I said, rubbing Eby's head as he snaked around my legs in a figure eight.

We'd just gone through the last room and extinguished the smudge stick in the kitchen sink, when the laundry room door burst open and Maddie bounced into the room. I hadn't heard the garage door open, I'd been so distracted. "What's that weird smell?" she asked, crinkling her nose like a rabbit.

Finn scooped her up in his arms, tickling under her chin. "It's my new cologne, baby girl, don't you like it?" Maddie was giggling so hard, she couldn't answer.

"What is that smell, Cain?" Mom asked, dropping her keys and purse on the counter.

"Um, Eby left me a litter box mess of epic proportions and it's a new air freshener I picked up somewhere." A perfectly believable excuse. Sometimes the smells emanating from Eby's litter box seemed otherworldly.

"It's very pleasant. Reminds me of the forest. Alright, Maddie, time for your bath and then bed."

Finn was still holding her, but she'd caught her breath from all the tickling. "Can't I stay up a little while longer? Please?"

"Don't you remember where we left off in the book last night? When the black dog dragged Ron under the Whomping Willow? The sooner you get in the bathtub, the sooner we can see what happens," I said.

"Oh! That's right! I'm going, Mom - see you in the bathroom!" Maddie wriggled out of Finn's arms, then scampered down the hallway.

"Thanks, Cain. Sometimes I wonder how long she'd go without bathing if I didn't force her every night," she chuckled. "Maddie and I already ate, but there are leftovers from last night in the fridge for you boys if you're hungry."

. . . . .

Half an hour later, after Finn and I had wolfed down leftover lasagna, Maddie was tucked into bed and we continued reading *The Prisoner of Azkaban*. When we'd been smudging the house, something had occurred to me. I'd only seen Sarah in the attic and my bedroom, but what if she'd been in other areas of the house? What if, God forbid, Maddie had seen her? If she had, I'd like to think Maddie would have said something, but she wasn't easily scared by things that disturbed other kids her age. She'd walked in on me watching horror movies more than once, and probably would have hidden and continued watching if I hadn't noticed and kicked her out.

It's not like Sarah could use Maddie the way she'd used me – I mean, as Sarah said, with my concussion, it was like throwing out a welcome mat for her to come on in and make herself at home. Maddie was just a little girl, and even if Sarah was able to take over Maddie's body, what could she do? It's not as if Maddie was in high school and Sarah would be able to spy on Jacob and Nathan. Apparently, Sarah didn't need someone else's body for her murderous errands now anyway. Still, I wouldn't put it past her to try and scare Maddie for her own deranged amusement.

"Maddie, I know some parts of this book can be a little dark for smaller kids, but have you had any bad dreams after we've read or imagined you saw things in your room?"

Maddie puckered her mouth, eyes rolling up and to her right, searching her memory. She was wearing pajamas from her current favorite movie, *Frozen*. She'd made me watch it with her every night for a week after the DVD came out, so I could probably recite it from memory. Fairy tale cartoons weren't really my thing but, I had to admit, Olaf was one cool snowman.

"Nope. I don't think I've had any bad dreams."

"And you haven't seen anything weird in your room?"

"Well, sometimes Eby is weird, the way he lays on his back with all his paws in the air. My friend, Kaitlyn, says only dogs are supposed to sleep like that, not cats."

"Yeah, he's strange sometimes, but I guess Kaitlyn hasn't been lucky enough to have a cat as awesome as Eby."

"She said he's fat, too, but I said he's just over-fluffy, right?"

"Right," I chuckled. Maybe Sarah, for whatever reason, hadn't been in this part of the house. "Maddie, if you have a bad dream or think you see something scary, you know you can come and get me, right? Any time something scares you."

Maddie got up on her knees and hugged me, her arms tight around my neck, and I held her close, her freshly washed hair smelling of oranges. "You're a pretty good big brother, Cain. Some of my friends say their brothers are mean to them, but I always say how nice you are to me."

"Thanks, Maddie." Geez, this kid was going to make me cry. "Alright, let's get you tucked in again." I pulled the covers up to her chin, kissed her on the forehead, and turned on her nightlight. "Love you, Maddie."

"Love you, too, Cain."

CHAPTER 24

I woke in the middle of the night in a cold sweat, pulse racing, with a deep in my gut certainty that something wasn't right. Raising my hand to my neck, I groped for the talisman, frantic it might have fallen off while I'd slept. Exhaling in relief, I gripped its hard, compact shape, warm from lying against my skin, and felt a small amount of comfort.

Surveying the room, I squinted at the corners draped in shadows, praying Sarah wasn't there. I noted the closed attic door, and she wasn't sitting on my bed, or standing at the foot of it glaring at me, as she had before. Finn was on the futon across the room and shifted in his sleep. Surprisingly, I could hear his soft snores over the blood rushing through my veins.

Unable to see anything out of the ordinary, I convinced myself it was only a nightmare that woke me, and my body was just confused. Then I heard her guttural voice.

"What did you do?" Sarah hissed.

I bolted upright in my bed, frantically searching for her, and in the back of my mind, I remembered how as a young boy, I'd always been terrified something was under my bed, waiting to grab my ankles with its icy, bony fingers, then pull me under the bed with it, as I kicked and screamed in horror. What if Sarah was under there, just waiting for me to try and leave the room? To preserve my sanity, part of my mind built a wall, insisting that scenario couldn't happen. The other, more twisted and creative section provided me brief flashes of all the ways Sarah could kill or torture me as I lived out my worst childhood fear.

Knowing that she was here somewhere, but being unable to find her was almost as unsettling as actually seeing her. Then I caught a flash of something in my peripheral vision, but had trouble grasping what I saw. Sarah was partially on the ceiling facing me, backed into the corner by my bedroom door, her legs pinned against the wall. The palms of her gray hands, appearing very solid now, were pressed to the wall as if holding her in place, her facial features twisted in anger. Waves of hatred rolled off her, threatening to drive me into the mattress, helpless against her.

"What did you do, Cain?" she hissed even louder.

Lunging for the nightstand, I fumbled for the lamp switch but, as my attention was on Sarah instead of watching what I was doing, only succeeded in toppling over the lamp, hearing the tinkling of the bulb breaking as it hit the floor. The switch to the overhead light was almost directly under Sarah, and no way was I getting that close to her, so I was stuck with only the faint light filtering through the window.

"Wh….what do you mean?" I stuttered, struggling to find my voice as I pushed myself against the headboard of my bed.

Shuffling from the other side of the room told me Finn was awake. "Mother of God," he croaked. And Finn wasn't a religious kind of guy.

"I'm bound to this corner and can't leave the house or go to the attic. What have you done to me!" she growled.

Wait, what was that off in the distance shining very faintly? Could it possibly be a glimmer of hope? Had the smudging really worked?

And then I noticed something that sent the twinge of hope galloping off into the sunset. Sarah had dark stains on her arms and backs of her hands, streaks that were never there before. While she was immobile and I was safe for the moment, I needed to know the truth. The question had to be asked. "Sarah, did you have anything to do with Liam's death?"

Her lips curved into a hideous smile, and I knew the truth without hearing her confirmation. She'd killed him, or had somehow been responsible for his death.

"Yes, Cain, I killed Liam, and he deserved it. Don't look so shocked. You had to know it was going to happen." She was gloating, radiant at taking Liam's life. My veins turned to ice, my body feeling cold deep to the core.

"He was stunned at first when he saw me in the rearview mirror of his car, and probably thought I was someone else. Someone alive. I was a little worried he'd have a coronary and ruin my evening. Liam didn't want to believe it was me at first, like he thought someone was playing a joke on him. But when he heard my voice telling him he was going to die, that he would pay for what he'd done to me, Liam realized I'd returned from the dead.

"And then he screamed! He actually screamed like a little girl!" Sarah screeched as if she'd just won the lottery, exhilarated at reliving Liam's last moments. The obvious pleasure she'd felt at his fear made me physically ill. "He ran off the road and tried to get out of the car, but I made sure the doors stayed locked. It was fun, playing with him like that before slicing his throat. Sure, I could have broken his neck and made it quick, but I wanted him to suffer. I stayed around and watched the blood shooting out of his carotid arteries before he died. Such a satisfying evening."

Rage hit me like a punch in the face to know that while Liam wasn't entirely innocent, Sarah thought so little about taking his life. "How could you do that? How could you stand there and watch him die a slow, horrific death? You deserve to burn in hell for what you did to him!"

Sarah struggled to free herself from whatever bound her to the ceiling and if looks could kill, I'd be belly up by now.

"You have no idea what you're talking about, Cain! You don't know what they did to me. Do you think I died from falling down the stairs? If I told you I was alive when they buried me, when I needed help, and that I'd regained consciousness long enough to realize what was happening to me, would that justify killing Liam?"

"No – they didn't. Wouldn't they have checked ….? How could they have….?" Finn couldn't complete a sentence. And I understood why.

Sarah had been buried alive. I couldn't begin to imagine the terror and helplessness she must have felt, knowing her life was ending and she would die alone. None of it would have happened if Jacob, Nathan, and Liam hadn't lied to her, tricked her into coming to this house. If they'd just done the responsible thing and called for help, owned up to what had happened, Sarah would still be alive and none of us would be living this hellish nightmare. Liam would still have his life and I wouldn't be fearing for my own.

"Do you think they'd have buried you if they'd known you were alive? They probably panicked and overlooked a pulse, assumed you were already dead and it was all an accident. I'm not defending them, what they did was beyond cruel, but you deliberately killed Liam, tortured him, and that's different."

Sarah was seething, her fury almost a separate, living thing. "I knew you'd take their side, Cain, you're just like them and that's why I tried to get

Lindsey to stay away from you. They deliberately pushed me down the stairs when they figured out no one was getting in my pants and thought they'd killed me! If they'd discovered I was still alive, they would have finished the job because they're cowards and only worried about their own fates. You're an idiot if you think it could have happened any other way. You can't run from your sins, and in the end, Liam knew that. Jacob and Nathan will learn it soon enough."

And there it was. It was one thing to think Sarah would probably try to kill Jacob and Nathan also, but hearing her confirm it and show no remorse for Liam was another.

"That's not for you to decide, Sarah, don't you see? You've lingered here because you believe they killed you, cheated you out of your life. But you're doing the same thing to them. And it's wrong."

"Where I am, there is no right or wrong, but knowing they suffered will at least give me some degree of peace. Don't look for any redeeming qualities in me, Cain. There aren't any left."

A feeling of calmness washed over me and in that moment, I wasn't afraid of her. Instead, I felt sorry for her. "Then we're done, Sarah. You used my body again, then murdered Liam. It's time for you to get out of my house and move on to wherever you should have gone in the first place. But after what you've done, I wouldn't expect a rainbow-filled afterlife."

At my words, Sarah glowed with hatred, her features purely demonic. "If you believe telling me to leave your house is all it takes – think again."

Mona had been right. It wouldn't be as easy as commanding her to leave – it had accomplished nothing. I should be grateful the smudging had some effect on Sarah and I still had the protection amulet until we either found her body or figured out another solution.

"At least we know you won't be out there trying to hurt anyone else tonight," Finn said.

"You know what they say about assumptions, Finn. I'm getting stronger every minute – I was here long before you could see me. Sleep well and know you'll be watched the rest of the night." Sarah's sinister expression held the promise of the torture I'd receive if she was free. "And don't even think about moving to another room. I'll find you wherever you are and I'm sure you don't want to endanger your family."

Sarah threatening Mom and Maddie was my worst nightmare, beyond any fear she'd instilled in me, and although I'd known it was a possibility, hearing her actually say it stopped me cold. Because I'd been planning to grab Finn and slip out the door underneath Sarah while she was still pinned against the ceiling, then sleep in another room. Instead, I'd be spending what was sure to be a sleepless night in my own bed as Sarah loomed overhead, never taking her dark, venomous gaze from me. Inching my way down, I lay prone in my bed, all the while staring at her blood-streaked hands and dead, ashen face, silently praying that if Sarah freed herself, my amulet would offer protection from certain death.

CHAPTER 25

"Finn, it would save time if we talked to Jacob and Nathan, warned them about Sarah, and then hope they tell us where her body is buried."

"After Sarah's midnight confessional, I'm with you on telling them she's on the loose and is probably, as we speak, googling the ten most effective torture methods she could use before murdering them, but you're delusional if you think they'll spill their guts about A, killing a girl, and two, where they hid the body. Then there's the small detail they overlooked about reporting it."

Finn and I were exhausted this morning after our all-night vigil. We'd both fallen asleep at some point, but Sarah was nowhere in sight when we woke, and Eby's warm body was curled up against me. Maybe the amulet had worked or Sarah had a hectic day of killing planned and couldn't spare the time to deal with me. Or maybe Eby had scared her away. Whatever the case, I was still alive.

"When they find out Sarah killed Liam, don't you think they'd want to tell us where the body is to save their own lives?" I asked, watching as Finn threw a ball of aluminum foil across the room and my less than graceful cat dived after it.

"You're assuming they'd believe your story about a ghost killing their friend based on what? I'll admit, those two aren't in any danger of exceeding the maximum intellectual capacity of humans, but two weeks ago, would you have believed a ghost with earth-shattering anger issues lived in your house? And planned on leaving a trail of bodies in her wake?"

"What's wrong with your cat? I thought they always landed on their feet," Finn said, after Eby jumped on my desk and lost his balance, falling to the floor in a tangle of legs and paws.

"Their agility is highly overrated. So how can we prove Sarah exists, short of getting them to spend the night and hope she shows up. Scratch that, she'd be able to take out all of us at once and make her job a lot easier."

"I don't know if it's possible to prove she exists. Maybe the best we can do is give them some details about that night only they would know, tell them their life expectancy may not be quite as long as they'd hoped, and leave it in their hands to believe us or not. I'm guessing it's a not, but it's worth a shot. If they 'fess up, at least we won't have to bushwhack your back yard trying to find a body."

No one could ever say Finn wasn't practical and brutally honest. Some of his previous girlfriends had learned not to ask if certain clothes made them look fat or if he liked their new hairstyle and he'd received his share of slaps across the face. His response? "Don't ask if you can't handle the truth, sweetheart."

"So, we go find Jacob and Nathan and tell them. Best case scenario, at least one of them will show us where Sarah is buried. Worst case scenario, we walk aimlessly around my yard and the woods behind and hope we trip over her grave."

. . . . .

Texting a few friends about Jacob's and Nathan's whereabouts led us to the beach, where they were playing football with some guys from the team. No big surprise there. When we'd made plans in my bedroom, confronting them had sounded like a good idea at the time, but now that we were here, I wondered if this was the best approach. Eight of them, two of us. Depending on how things went, people could be searching for our graves in the near future.

Jacob saw us approaching and called out. "Are you two taking a romantic walk on the beach together or did you come here to learn how to play a real sport?"

"We'll talk about a real sport when you can run nonstop for a forty-five minute half. They don't have huddles and time-outs in soccer, Jacob," Finn smirked. When it came to football versus soccer, friendly rivalry was just code for battling testosterone levels. We meant every word we said, just as they did.

"Can we talk to you and Nathan?" I asked. Jacob nodded and declared a break, while the other players jogged down to the water.

Jacob and Nathan trudged through the sand, Jacob kicking some in

Finn's direction as he sat down. I doubted it was an accident, but Finn chose not to retaliate, settling for glowering at Jacob instead. I'm not a fan of having sand up my shorts, but when you live by the beach, it's a part of life and you learn to live with it.

"Sorry about Liam. I know you guys have been friends for a while," I said, offering condolences in hopes of starting off in a neutral zone. But I really was sorry about what had happened to Liam. I wouldn't wish that on anyone.

"Yeah, thanks, Cain. That was really screwed up what happened to him," Jacob said, although he seemed to be more interested in three girls wearing swimsuits walking along the shoreline.

"The cops questioned all of us to see if we had any ideas about who could have done that to him, but none of us were any help. Liam didn't have any enemies, so I'm thinking it was some random psycho," Nathan added. "He'd just dropped us off about ten minutes earlier and was nearly home."

At least Nathan seemed a little more human and showed genuine concern for Liam. Jacob was still watching the girls, but at Nathan's words, he jumped in the conversation.

"Hey, it wasn't our fault he couldn't fight off some serial killer or whoever did that to him. No way would someone have taken me out like that. There might have been a dead body, but I guarantee it wouldn't have been mine," Jacob said, leaning back and puffing out his well-defined chest.

"I'm sensing you're not deep in the throes of grief, Jacob. Don't you give a crap about what happened to Liam?" Finn and I agreed Jacob had the emotional capacity of a gummy bear, but Finn wasn't making this any easier by calling him on it.

Jacob's hands clenched as he leaned into Finn's personal space. "You don't know anything about how I feel, Finn. Did you come here to start something with me? You need to put a muzzle on your friend, Cain."

Finn's whole body tensed as if he was ready to spring. This wasn't going at all like I'd planned. "Look, Jacob, Finn doesn't mean anything by it. We came here to tell you something and want to help you."

Nathan had been silent during the exchange between Jacob and Finn, but his forehead creased at that comment. "Do you know something about what happened to Liam?"

Taking a deep breath, I began. "Yeah, I know who killed Liam, but you probably won't believe me and should try to keep an open mind. Finn and I don't agree with what you did, but don't want to see either of you end up like Liam."

"Well, thanks for not wishing us dead, Cain, but get to the point and tell us what you're yapping about," Jacob snapped.

"We know what happened with the three of you and Sarah Butler." Nathan's head jerked toward Jacob, who'd probably make an excellent poker player, because the only tell on him was the flaring of his nostrils. "We know it happened at my house while it was being built, and somehow Sarah didn't come out alive. Her ghost is there and she's responsible for killing Liam."

For several moments, the only sounds were the seagulls overhead, the crashing of the waves, and laughter from the other guys as they body surfed. I wondered if Jacob and Nathan had heard me, or even understood what I'd said.

And then Jacob barked out a laugh that sounded more like a donkey braying. "Come on, Cain. Is this some stupid joke you made up to get back at me for going out with Erin? She traded up for me when she dumped you, dude, get over it."

Jacob might have been cracking jokes, but Nathan's face was whiter than the sand we sat on and his lips trembled slightly.

Finn snorted. "You're with Erin now? There's a certain symmetry in that, I guess, since you both deserve each other. Oh, and Erin didn't dump Cain. YouTube doesn't lie."

"Whatever, Finn. If you guys are finished, I've got better things to do. Sorry if I disappointed you by not playing along with your joke, but I'm smarter than that," Jacob said, standing and dusting the sand off his shorts.

"Don't kid yourself, Jacob. You're really not."

Jacob's jaw clenched and the muscles in his forearms flexed. I jumped to my feet to head off Jacob and Finn before they started something. "Come on, guys, just stop for a minute. Nathan, you alright?" His arms were wrapped tightly around his knees, chin resting of top of them, and he flinched when I touched his shoulder to get his attention.

"Yeah. Yeah, I'm fine." Which was the exact opposite of how he appeared.

"Look, I know you may not believe in ghosts, but I've spoken to Sarah and she's been scaring the crap out of me almost daily for the past few weeks. She told me how the three of you invited her to some fake party at my house to win a bet. Once she figured it out, she tried to leave and thinks one of you pushed her down the stairs.

"You thought she was dead, so you panicked and buried her somewhere. There are so many things wrong about that, I don't know where to begin, but the biggest problem is that Sarah wasn't dead when you buried her. She was still alive."

"And now she's back, completely deranged, with a temper of epic proportions, and you two are the next items on her to-do list, so you might want to listen to us," Finn added.

Nathan didn't seem to be breathing and had a wild air about him, like he was ready to bolt. If there had been any doubt in my mind about Sarah's story being true, Nathan's reaction ruled it out. Jacob would deny everything until the end because he'd only ever been concerned about number one.

"Are you two freaks serious? Not only are you accusing us of murdering some girl I've never heard of, but you're saying a ghost told you all of this? And she's coming to kill us? I think you'd better take this wacked out story and get out of my sight before I hurt you both."

"But Jacob, what if she…"

"Not another word, Nathan!" Jacob snapped.

"Think about it, Jacob. How would Cain and I know anything about what happened between the four of you?"

Nathan grabbed Jacob's arm, his knuckles white as he pleaded. "Jacob, I think we should listen…"

Jacob tugged his arm from Nathan's grip. "Nathan, I said not another word! We're leaving. I don't want to hear any more of this crap. Get up and let's go." Jacob grasped Nathan's upper arm, jerked him to a standing position and shoved him in the direction of their other friends, who were now watching us from a distance, interested in the cause of Jacob's shouting. Jacob stalked away and Nathan stumbled through the sand following him, but cast a backwards glance at us.

"When she comes for you, you'll wish you'd listened to us!" Finn yelled. Jacob's reply was carried away in the ocean breeze, but I read lips well enough to get the gist of it - and he wasn't thanking us. "Not that I'm condoning murder in any way, but you can kind of see how Jacob's attitude could make even a sane person lean in that direction, you know?"

"Yeah. But I think we've found our weak link in Nathan," I replied, sliding in the passenger seat of Finn's car. "Maybe if we got him away from Jacob, he'd help us. When I mentioned Sarah's name, he looked like her ghost had sat down in the sand beside him."

"I don't think we'll have to worry about trying to get Nathan away from Jacob. I'll bet you a triple bacon cheeseburger he comes to us on his own. The guy looked scared out of his mind," Finn said, pulling into traffic.

"That should make things a little easier for a change."

CHAPTER 26

With Mom and Maddie home this evening, I wasn't able to trek through the house with the smudge stick, but that didn't stop me from lighting it in my room. I just hoped Mom didn't smell anything and accuse me of smoking weed. But I was pretty sure she knew the difference between burning herbs, wood, and pot. Despite her assurances she'd never given her parents any problems when growing up, grandma had told me Mom was no angel.

No sign of Sarah, but I theorized the smudging yesterday might have weakened her a little and she was staying away to conserve her energy. At least that's what I was telling myself. Sarah being weak might be the only thing standing between life and death for Nathan or Jacob tonight. Thinking about Liam's horrific death made me notice I'd been absent-mindedly rubbing my thumb across the protective amulet Mona had given me. Maybe we could get a couple more for Nathan and Jacob, although I questioned whether Jacob would wear his. Nathan might wear both of them for double protection.

The ding of my phone a little after midnight let me know I had a new text. When I saw who it was from, I briefly closed my eyes in relief. Finn had called it. The text was from Nathan and he wanted to meet with us, but it had to be kept from Jacob. No surprise there. If Jacob had possessed duck tape on the beach, he would have used it on Nathan to keep him quiet about the secrets the two of them were keeping.

Bringing Nathan to this house was out of the question – he'd never make it across the threshold. A dead body, not to mention the high likelihood of blood spatter, would get Mom's attention, with the odds overwhelmingly against the police buying my story about a ghost being responsible. My future would consist of numerous psych evaluations and therapists for many years to come.

Meeting in a public place wouldn't give us a lot of privacy, especially if

Nathan started freaking out, so I decided Finn's house was the best option. After letting Nathan know I'd get back to him about a meeting place, I started dialing Finn's number, but then stopped. What if Sarah was listening? For all I knew, she might have been looking over my shoulder while I texted Nathan, but I felt like if she was, the room temperature would have dropped. Would she have to be in the same room to listen to me? Could she hear from the attic – if that's where she was right now?

Texting seemed like the smartest choice, so after a few back and forths, we decided on meeting tomorrow after Liam's funeral. Nathan said he'd get away from Jacob and be there. By this time tomorrow, we might know the truth about what happened and where Sarah's body was buried and put this whole nightmare behind us. I hoped.

. . . . .

School was a pretty grim place Monday morning. Several girls were crying. Some were Liam's friends, but I wondered if the others even knew him. There were always people who lived for the drama. Although Jacob hadn't seemed too broken up about Liam's death, most of the football players were pretty somber, many of them wearing black arm bands. One guy had even shaved Liam's jersey number into his head. Grief counselors were available and the funeral was scheduled for two hours after school to give students enough time to attend.

Stalking me seemed to be Jacob's new hobby because every time I turned a corner in the hallway at school, he was there, leering at me. When I went downstairs to chemistry class, there he was again. From the way he kept appearing out of nowhere, I wondered if he was a ghost too, or just an experienced stalker. Maybe he'd had practice with Sarah. I'd hoped to catch Nathan alone and find out where Sarah's body was buried before we met later, but Jacob made sure that wasn't a possibility.

Nathan looked even worse than he did yesterday, with dark circles under his eyes and a rumpled appearance. His posture was slumped and he kept looking over his shoulder, like he expected someone - or something - to be following him. I could empathize. Sleep and I hadn't been very good friends lately, but I'd become well-acquainted with fear.

. . . . .

Lunch in the cafeteria was kind of unidentifiable, although I think it was some sort of greenish-gray meat. Maybe. The cottage cheese might have been the smartest way to go after all.

"Couldn't you have just asked Nathan to text you the location of the, um, dig last night? My thinking is the sooner we have that location the better," Finn said, poking at his food as if checking for signs of life.

"I mentioned it, but he didn't want to put that kind of information on his phone. It's pretty incriminating stuff."

"Guess that makes sense." Finn had abandoned the meat thing for the nonthreatening french fries, although he kept glancing back at it like he expected a surprise attack.

Lindsey slid into the chair beside me and my day got a little brighter, then approached supernova when she leaned over and kissed me.

"Hey, you. How did things go yesterday? It's horrible what happened to Liam – to die like that. I can't put it into words. And his parents – just unbelievably sad. We're thinking this was Sarah, right?"

Finn dropped his spork and gave me an incredulous stare. "You didn't tell her?"

"Didn't tell me what? Did I miss something else?" Lindsey asked, her head swiveling between the two of us.

Before I could answer, Finn did it for me. "Now two people may be gunning for your little stud muffin here. Well, one person and one ghost. Guess it just depends on who gets to him first, but I don't think that protective amulet can help him much with Jacob, unless he stabs him in the eye with it. Whether it works on Sarah is still a gray area, too."

Lindsey grabbed my forearm, gripping it tightly. "She threatened you? Cain, why didn't you tell me?"

Stupid Finn. The corner of his mouth twitched as he portrayed the perfect picture of innocence. "I didn't want to worry you this weekend. You had enough on your mind with the state orchestra tryouts coming up. And it's not like she could have done anything to me, because she was a little incapacitated at the time, thanks to Mona's smudge stick."

"So, it helped," she said, relaxing her hold. "But what about when the effects wear off? What happens then?"

I shrugged. "I honestly don't know, Lindsey. Guess it all depends on the amulet. Besides, Sarah seems more concerned with Jacob and Nathan right now. After that, who knows what will happen unless we find her body?"

"I'm seeing Aunt Mona after the funeral today. Do you need anything else from her?"

"Could you get an amulet for Nathan? I guess one for Jacob too, but I doubt he'd even take it. Maybe it would give Nathan some peace of mind just wearing it. We could give it to him this evening when we meet at Finn's."

"Sure. Maybe I should get a couple for Finn and me, too."

"I figured that was a done deal. The two of you wearing them would give *me* some peace of mind."

. . . . .

As I rounded the corner on my way to the last class of the day, someone grabbed the back of my shirt and pulled me into a dimly lit supply closet. My books fell to the floor as I was jerked around, then shoved against the wall. And found myself face to face with Jacob.

"What's your problem, Jacob?" I asked, shoving him back.

"Shut up, Shannon! I don't know why you'd invent that wacked out story you told yesterday, but you'd better not be spreading it around. Nathan's all freaked out that you'll tell someone and get us both in trouble, so keep it to yourself, got that?"

"What makes you think I'd tell people something like that? You still think I've got some personal vendetta against you? You're wrong - I don't care if you're dating Erin. I'm better off without her, believe me. I only told you about Sarah to protect you."

"Protect me? From something that doesn't even exist? Look, Shannon, I didn't even know the girl and if I hear you accusing me of doing anything to her, maybe you'll be the one found at the side of the road."

"I could bring up how it wouldn't be your first time killing someone...." He lunged toward me, fist raised. "Just hang on and listen, Jacob!" I said, pushing him back. "But what I have to say may save your life, so give me the benefit of the doubt."

When he didn't punch me right away, I hoped it meant he was considering his options. Maybe he was smarter than Finn thought.

He lowered his fist and leaned back against the wall. "Fine. I'll listen, but that doesn't mean I believe you."

"Jacob, I've seen Sarah and she's a walking nightmare. While she was pinned to my ceiling, watching me all night, she told me in detail what happened to Liam. And she's not finished. She's seen you and Nathan, how you've gone on with your lives and shown no remorse.

"Finn and I have talked to people and researched our options and unless we find her body, I don't know if she can be stopped. You may think all this sounds insane, but if you'd lived through and seen what I had over the past couple of weeks, you'd be dragging me to where she's buried instead of threatening me. We need to know where Sarah is, pour salt on her remains, and burn them. If that doesn't happen, she'll kill you and Nathan, but only after you've experienced indescribable pain."

With the murky light in the closet, it was hard to be sure, but Jacob's coloring seemed kind of ashy and the tendons in his neck stood out. He raised his hand and stabbed his finger into my chest. "You're crazy, Cain. You and Finn stay away from me." Then he flung open the door and stomped out.

Jacob could deny everything, threaten me and call me delusional, but I wasn't fooled. Before he'd touched me, I'd seen his unsteady hand and heard his wavering voice. Jacob was scared.

CHAPTER 27

Did it make me a horrible person to wish I'd never come to Liam's funeral? With the sudden loss of my Dad last year, it's not like death and I were unacquainted. I'd also lost my grandmother to cancer a couple of years ago and then my grandpa had a heart attack just last year. My grandmother had been sick for a long time and we knew she wouldn't be with us much longer, and my grandpa was old, stubborn and wouldn't give up the cigarettes and take care of himself, so their deaths hadn't been unexpected.

Liam's funeral was completely different and I hoped to never experience this again. Now I understood what they meant when people said parents should never have to bury their children.

A heavy cloud of grief hung over all those in attendance. Liam's mother cried through the entire service - not silent crying into a tissue, but agonizing, gut-wrenching sobs that made me feel as if we were all intruding on a private moment. His father sat beside her, arm around her shoulder, but his eyes were glazed over and distant, making me think he'd been medicated. Liam's younger sister sat by herself, head lowered, legs kicking back and forth, her parents' anguish so great they were incapable of consoling her.

Liam's teammates were there and many of them tried to hide their tears, but some weren't embarrassed at all to be seen crying for the loss of their friend. I would never, ever wish this kind of torment on my worst enemy. Just the thought of Mom experiencing something like this with Maddie or me felt like someone had reached inside me and twisted my internal organs.

Sarah was responsible for all the grief, pain, and sadness here - the loss of a son, a brother, and a friend. This was something his parents would never get over. Not only was Liam dead, he'd been murdered and they'd probably never learn the identity of his killer. Even if they were told Sarah took their only son from them, they'd never believe it or be able to accept it. All this misery and fear because of a testosterone-fueled bet that went off the rails and shredded the lives of so many people.

On the other side of the grave, directly across from me, I saw Jacob's defiant stare, with no trace of fear now as he slowly shook his head. I assumed that was his way of reminding me to keep my craziness away from him and Nathan.

Wait - Nathan. I didn't remember seeing him here, but he'd mentioned earlier he would be at the funeral. I scanned the crowd frantically, trying not to panic, thinking maybe Nathan had been too upset or scared to attend. He could be holed up in his bedroom hiding under the covers for all I knew. I continued searching the grieving masses, knowing how easy it would be to overlook him and almost believed that was possible - until I caught a glimpse of Sarah, partially visible behind a group of tearful girls, her gruesome smile victorious.

• • • • • • • •

Nathan was missing. In the rec room of Finn's house, I paced between the mini kitchen and window with a view of the driveway, checking my phone every thirty seconds for messages. He should have been here two hours ago and we'd heard nothing from him.

"Did he text back yet?"

"No, Finn, he hasn't responded to any of my fifteen texts, ten voice mails, and twenty-two calls," I growled, knowing none of this was Finn's fault, but still barking at him. Lindsey had dropped off the protection amulets earlier and offered to stay, but I knew she had orchestra tryouts this weekend. Besides, I was a little unbearable to be around this evening. But that hadn't stopped her from kissing me senseless before she'd left.

"You know, Cain, strutting around here like a model on the runway isn't helping the situation," Finn said, lounging on the couch and flipping through a *Sports Illustrated* magazine.

How he could be so calm was beyond my comprehension. Even if it was last year's swimsuit issue. "What if he's dead? What if she's torturing him right now? We've got a protection amulet for him and it's useless. We're too late."

Finn tossed the magazine on the table, then went to the mini fridge and took out two bottles of water. "We don't know for sure if that's what happened – not at the moment anyway, unless Sarah turns up to gloat again."

He tossed one of the bottles to me. "Take a seat and let's talk about what we know."

It had always been this way for us, balancing each other. His parents' divorce, my Dad's death. When one of us freaked out, the other became more calm and rational. More evidence we acted like an old married couple. I flopped down on the couch and cracked open the bottle of water, drinking half of it in one swig.

"I think we should ask Jacob if he knows where Nathan is," Finn said.

"Yeah, that's the logical thing to do. But what if Nathan is with him and can't get away? I'd hate to see him in trouble with Jacob because of us. I don't care what Jacob does to me, I can hold my own with him, but it seems like Nathan goes along with whatever he says."

"I really think if he was with Jacob, he would have found a way to text us or make an excuse and get away from him, don't you? Go to the restroom and text, it's simple. Even if he's not with Jacob, maybe Jacob knows where he is. We're not getting anything done by sitting here waiting."

After texting Jacob a few times with no reply, I decided to call. If he was annoyed enough, maybe he'd answer the phone to shut me up. Or block my number.

On the third try, he finally answered.

"What do you want, Shannon? What part of keep your crazy away from me didn't you understand?"

"Is Nathan with you?"

"Seriously? This is what you're calling me about? Text him you.."

"Jacob, this is serious," I interrupted. "I need to know if he's with you or if you've seen him today."

I heard Jacob muttering to himself, curses directed at me, mostly. "No, Cain, I haven't seen him, alright? He was the only player who missed the funeral and hasn't gotten back to me since after school. After hearing all that trash you've been spouting about some ghost coming after us, he's probably hiding under his bed like a wuss."

Pounding my fist against the wall in frustration, I tried to get him to listen. "Look, Jacob, Nathan was supposed to meet me at Finn's house this evening. I know you don't believe me about Sarah, but I saw her at the funeral today and with Nathan missing, I'm afraid she may have gotten to him."

"Wait, you're telling me you saw a ghost at the funeral today? Seems like if some dead person was walking around, someone else might have noticed, don't you think?"

Punching the wall wasn't enough. My fist ached to connect with Jacob's face. "I don't know why only I could see her, but that's not the issue, Jacob. We have protection amulets for both you and Nathan. That's one of the reasons he was coming here tonight. We were hoping he'd also tell us where Sarah is buried so we can get rid of her and maybe save your miserable life."

"And don't think we haven't had second thoughts about that!" Finn yelled, loud enough for Jacob to hear him and toss back some choice words of his own.

"I've had enough of this, and I'm done. I don't know where Nathan is, but some imaginary ghost isn't the reason he wasn't at the funeral. You and your freak of nature friend have him scared and he's probably hiding. If he said he knows something about a grave, that's on him, but don't go accusing me of killing someone and hiding a body. And don't bother me with this again!"

He hung up on me – not unexpected, but now we knew Nathan wasn't with him and Jacob hadn't seen him or talked to him since school today. And that didn't speak well for the status of Nathan's life right now.

"He called you a freak of nature."

Finn tilted his head to the side and pondered those words for a moment. "I wouldn't necessarily take that as an insult. Freaks of nature can be pretty awesome sometimes."

"He hasn't seen Nathan."

"I figured as much. Maybe we should both go to your room and wait for Sarah to show up – see if this protection bling really works."

"Are you sure you want to do that? With the way she looked the other night, seeing her again could do some serious psychological damage. Even a mother couldn't love that face."

"Eh – who isn't psychologically damaged in some way or other, right? I've got your back, you've got mine."

CHAPTER 28

Finn and I waited for Sarah, even called out for her. After playing video games for two hours, eating most of two pizzas, and binge-watching four episodes of *Supernatural*, there was still no sign of her. No room temperature changes, attic doors opening, or otherworldly creatures stuck on my ceiling. Even Eby stayed in the room with us, but that was probably because Finn kept feeding him bites of pepperoni. Even if Sarah was here, the pepperoni might have motivated Eby to stay.

If she'd done something to Nathan, she'd want to gloat about it and share all the gory details, maybe even bring back a trophy of some sort. Sarah didn't kill quietly. She preferred to play with her food first, aim for shock value, and make a statement. Ironically, that's the opposite of when she was alive, hiding in the background and avoiding drawing attention to herself.

We finally called it a night around 2 am. Eby curled up with me on my bed and Finn settled in his usual spot on the futon. An hour later, we were awakened by a piercing screech, like fingernails clawing down a chalkboard.

"What have you done! Why can't I touch you!"

Being woken by Sarah in the middle of the night was becoming routine and I immediately shot up in bed. In the dim light, I saw Finn go from prone to a crouched, defensive position in the blink of an eye. As a keeper, he'd always had quick reflexes, and his eyes darted around the room, seeking the threat. Even Eby was caught unaware and leapt at Sarah as he sprinted from the room.

When I'd first seen Sarah, she'd been nearly opaque, but with normal human mannerisms and as long as a person was comfortable being around a ghost, she really hadn't been that threatening. The Sarah that stood in front of me was truly macabre, her skin a sickening greenish-gray, with inky, dark shadows lining her face. Long tendrils of slimy-looking hair fell in limp strands that snaked over her shoulders.

And her cold, cadaverous hands were again streaked with dried blood.

The color drained from Finn's face as he gaped at Sarah.

She launched herself toward me, her feet hovering several inches above the floor, but came to an abrupt stop about six feet away, almost as if she'd smacked into a brick wall, and her lips drew back in a snarl.

"What have you done?" she screeched again. "There's something glowing around you, like a wall!"

That didn't stop her from trying. Sarah charged at me from every angle, but the protection amulet did what Mona had promised. Too bad the barrier wasn't like those invisible fences for dogs, shocking Sarah every time she hit it.

"It's called a protection amulet, you decaying psychopath, and it's to keep devil spawn like you away from him. Seems to be pretty effective, doesn't it?" Finn had recovered from the shock of Sarah's appearance, but taunting her couldn't lead to anything good. Her head snapped in his direction, as if she'd forgotten Finn was here. In her frustration over her failed attempts to reach me, it was possible Sarah hadn't noticed Finn.

Her lips parted, mouth twisting into a cruel grimace, and in the dim light, it resembled an empty black void.

"Oh, it's you, Finn," Sarah said in a dismissive voice.

"Wouldn't be the first time a woman was disappointed to see me, although you're the first dead one who felt that way." Finn had gotten up from his crouched position and was inching toward my desk.

Sarah turned toward Finn, drifting in his direction. "Do you always joke when you're nervous? Trying to hide the fact that you probably need a change of underwear right about now?"

With Finn leaning against my desk, arms across his chest and legs crossed at the ankles, he looked entirely too casual, considering he was talking to a vengeful, murdering ghost who was probably running game plays through her mind about the different ways she'd like to kill us right now. "If the joking bothers you, I could say what I'm really thinking. Like how I'd love to send you straight to hell where you belong and how much pleasure it would give me to rid the world of you. Is that better?"

Sarah's face contorted into a picture of dark rage at Finn's words. A gauzy, gray mist appeared, slowly rising around her, swirling from her feet up along her torso, as if she were gathering her energy, then she surged at Finn, arms outstretched, lank strands of hair streaming behind her. Seeing Sarah threaten Finn gave me a burst of energy that propelled me out of bed in their direction, but my help wasn't needed. Sarah stopped cold a couple of feet from Finn, and she howled in frustration. I made a mental note to grovel at Mona's feet in gratitude the next time we met. Assuming I ever had the opportunity.

"I guess your afterlife sucks right about now, doesn't it?" Finn asked. He must have nerves of steel and complete faith in the talisman, because he hadn't even twitched when Sarah charged at him. "Now, what did you do to Nathan?"

Sarah slithered away from Finn, back toward the attic door that opened for her as she approached. Even though she'd just suffered a humiliating defeat in her attempts to terrorize us, her expression was triumphant.

"Nathan? What makes you think I'd know where Nathan is?" she asked. The fact that Sarah feigned innocence, and not well, made my blood boil.

"Come on, Sarah, I saw you at the funeral today and no one has seen Nathan since school. Did you hurt him? Can we help him at all or is it too late?" The blood on her hands led me to believe it was the latter, but I didn't want to give up hope just yet.

"Lose the jewelry and I'll tell you everything you need to know, Cain."

Almost unconsciously, my hands drifted toward the leather cord around my neck, and I glanced at Finn. He slowly shook his head. "Don't even think about it. You know she'd kill you the second she got a chance." He was right. Of course, he was right. What was I thinking?

Then Sarah was gone, remnants of the swirling mist all that remained of her. The attic door slammed hard enough to crack the frame, and I heard a menacing laugh echoing in the distance.

Finn and I stared at each other in the deafening silence of the aftermath of Hurricane Sarah. I exhaled loudly. "How did you know your talisman would work?"

Finn was bent over, hands on his knees. "I didn't. Yours worked and I prayed mine would too, but let's just say there was some shrinkage in certain parts of my anatomy when she came toward me and leave it at that."

I nodded and fell back onto the bed. "He's dead, you know."

"Yeah. I'm sure she killed him after he went through some excruciating pain, but there's nothing we can do."

Finn had returned to the futon and we both lay quietly. My thoughts flitted between Nathan and his probable murder, the questionable length of my own life span, and the chances of becoming a certified exorcist online. Neither of us would be getting much rest tonight.

"How do you do it, Cain?"

"What?"

"How do you stay in this room every night and sleep, knowing she's here, maybe even invisible and at your side watching, able to massacre you at any time?"

"She can find me wherever I am, so it doesn't make a difference. If I stay in my room, at least I know she'll be here, away from Mom and Maddie. Right now, this talisman is the most important thing I own and if I lost it....let's just say parts of *my* anatomy would shrink or I'd lose them permanently and leave it at that."

"Understood."

The next day, Nathan was all over the news. The unsolved murder of one football player and the disappearance of another in less than a week caused a frenzy of gossip among the students. Groups were clustered in hallways, classrooms, and the cafeteria whispering, crying, speculating, accusing, and spouting ridiculous theories about what might have happened.

One rumor had a jealousy-riddled Nathan killing Liam over a girl they were both in love with and Nathan had disappeared, taking the object of their affection with him. Except neither of them had girlfriends. Another had the two of them in love with each other, and after Liam's death, a grief-stricken Nathan had left town, too bereft to tell anyone where he was going. Except neither of them were gay.

I'd hoped Nathan's disappearance would convince Jacob to take us seriously and cooperate, but he didn't acknowledge my presence all day, ignoring my existence. If he was worried or concerned at all, he hid it well.

Finn, Lindsey, and I planned to scour my yard and the forest behind it for Sarah's grave after school today. Without Jacob's help, we'd be searching for a four leaf clover on a soccer field, but what other choice did we have? She was on a rampage and once she took care of Jacob, I could be her next target.

When Lindsey got to my house that afternoon, Eby was trotting around my legs, trying to herd me toward the pantry where his food stayed. Finn was still at practice and wouldn't be there for at least another hour. Opening the door and seeing that dazzling smile of hers put all grisly thoughts of Sarah out of my mind for the time being.

"Hey, you."

"Hey," I said, pulling her against me and wrapping my arms around her as our lips met –something that was becoming entirely natural to me. Then Lindsey pushed against my chest.

"Cain, what about your mom?"

I grinned broadly. "No one's home and Finn won't be here for another hour, so we have the house to ourselves."

"And you expect me to believe this is just a happy coincidence? That you didn't plan this?"

"Um....yes?" She laughed as I led her over to the couch, where we spent the next hour in a tangle of arms and lips and I found out exactly how it felt to leave a trail of kisses down her neck and over the delicate silver necklace she wore, now accompanied by her protection amulet.

"I guess it's true what they say about a common fear drawing people closer together. Really close, I guess. Don't let me interrupt. Should I sit down and wait for you?"

Finn. He'd used his key and since I'd been otherwise occupied with Lindsey, I hadn't heard him come in. We fumbled through straightening clothes and running hands through rumpled hair as we sat up, Lindsey's face a deep shade of scarlet as she burrowed against my neck in embarrassment.

"Have I ever told you what an ass you are, Finn?"

"Um, that would make the count somewhere around five hundred times. For this year, anyway. So, are we going grave hunting or what?"

CHAPTER 29

The odds of Sarah being buried somewhere within my fenced-in backyard were about as likely as Finn becoming politically correct overnight. One of us would have noticed it during our many hours of mowing, pruning, and trimming and if there was a grave to be found in the yard, it would have happened months ago. We did a quick sweep anyway, just to make sure all bases were covered, but nothing looked suspicious.

Beyond the fence, however, was an entirely different story. Several acres of wooded land and marsh separated our neighborhood from the one behind us. If you were in the market to hide a body, you could do a lot worse than this place.

"I don't even know where to begin. The grave could be anywhere," Lindsey said, as the three of us stared at the large expanse of land we needed to cover.

"I googled 'how to find a grave' and there really wasn't much to help us, but one website suggested using a metal detector. If Sarah was wearing some kind of jewelry, it would be picked up by the detector and save us some time."

"Well, that sounds like a great idea, Finn, if we actually had a metal detector. Which we don't," I said, wiping sweat from my forehead.

"Yes, we do, Cain. Guess I got so distracted by you and Lindsey making out, thinking about how I'd have to bleach my eyeballs to rid myself of that image, that I left it in the car. I borrowed our neighbor's metal detector. You know, Mrs. Kirby next door. She's always combing the beach with that thing thinking she'll find some buried treasure or something. Want me to get it?"

Over the next several hours, we swung the metal detector side to side as we trudged over a third of the land we needed to cover. Some areas we ruled out because of large rocks, root systems of massive trees, and marshy areas that would make digging or keeping a body in the ground nearly impossible. If the remains had managed to resurface, it wouldn't be a pretty sight.

By the end of the evening, we were tired, sweaty, and dirty, with only a few empty beer cans and some coins to show for our efforts. But the mosquitos had been thrilled to have us over for dinner.

"I've got a better idea," said Finn, leaving a trail of dirt when he wiped his forehead with his dirt-crusted hand. "Why don't we kidnap Jacob and torture him for the location of the grave. It's got to be easier than this. Who's with me?"

Lindsey raised her hand. Blonde strands of hair were plastered against her sweaty face and neck. After spending hours in the damp humidity, no closer to finding Sarah's body, Finn's suggestion was tempting. Very tempting. Especially since Nathan might still be alive if Jacob had cooperated with us.

"Alright," I said, leaning against the shovel. "Let's call it a night and we'll come up with some way to get Jacob to talk."

"Waterboarding? Seemed to be pretty effective when Jack Bauer from 24 used it. Just sayin'," Finn offered.

"At this point, I'm willing to consider anything," I said.

. . . . .

After showering, I planned to relax with an hour of mind-numbing television, then bunking on the couch downstairs for some much-needed sleep. Being out in the humidity all evening and digging around in the woods had completely wiped me out and my body felt like cinderblocks were tied to it.

I'd thought about watching TV downstairs, but with the late hour, Mom and Maddie were already asleep and I didn't want to wake them. Finally locating the remote under the clothes on my bed, I flicked on the SyFy channel, flopped onto one of the gamer chairs, and watched a rerun of the first *Sharknado* movie, perfect for zoning out. Eby wandered in to see if he was missing anything exciting, pawed at the television screen for a bit, rubbed against my leg, then sauntered out. Guess my life was too boring for him at the moment.

I'd just gotten to the part where the guy with the chainsaw gets himself swallowed by the shark, when I caught movement out of the corner of my eye and assumed Eby had come back. Turning to say something to him, I saw how very wrong I was.

Sarah was crawling out from under my bed, coming straight for me. She moved faster than any living thing I'd ever seen, but the disjointed, jerky movements of her body were completely inhuman. With the inky strands of hair trailing over her shoulders, gaunt shadows under her eyes and gray pallor of her skin, she would never be mistaken for anything living. She cocked her head sideways, a twisted smile contorting her features.

For one brief moment, I remembered Sarah couldn't touch me while I was wearing the protection amulet and my hand frantically groped for it, needing more than anything the feeling of comfort it provided.

It was gone.

With a stabbing sensation in my chest, I remembered I hadn't noticed it while showering and realized it must have fallen off while Lindsey and I were on the couch or worse, outside somewhere when we were digging. God help me, I wasn't safe and she was coming for me.

Flipping out of the gamer chair, I hurled my body toward the window, although I didn't know what I'd do when I got there, but needed to keep some distance between us. My hands groped through the piles of trash and clothes littering my floor, seeking anything that could help me, something I could use to defend myself. I located one of my soccer shoes and threw it at her, but it might as well have been a pillow for all the good it did. With my back against the wall under the window, there was nowhere else to go.

The last time she'd had me in this position, Sarah had been sitting on my bed, beautiful in an otherworldly way as the moonlight hovered around her. I'd been unsure of her intent, but fooled into believing she needed help. Sarah had played to my sympathies, said what I'd needed to hear, and deceived me all along while waiting for an opportunity to retaliate. Now, I was at her mercy and knew in the depths of my soul she wouldn't show me any.

She stopped a couple of feet in front of me and sat up, one leg splayed out in front of her, the other bent to the side and behind her at an unnatural angle, and she made a strangled sort of cackling sound that might have been a laugh.

"What's wrong, Cain? Paying the price now for that roll on the couch with your girlfriend? I was there watching, you know. I knew exactly when your ridiculous amulet fell down into the cushions. It's just like a guy to forget about everything else when he's thinking with the head that's not on his shoulders." Sarah's voice had changed, now raspy and gravelly, exactly how I'd imagined something from beyond the grave would sound.

"D-d-don't hurt me, Sarah. I haven't done anything to you. I was only trying to protect myself and my friends," I begged. The sound of my heartbeat thrashed in my ears and my stomach clenched, threatening to purge its contents.

"Hurt you?" she asked, her eyes wide, as if she were surprised at my request. "I'm not going to hurt you, Cain." The meager twinge of relief I felt was short-lived when she added, "Yet."

Now I knew for certain what my future held, as far as Sarah was concerned. When she was finished with Jacob, I'd be next. Or maybe Jacob was already slaughtered at the side of the road or in his own bed in a way that involved copious amounts of blood, pain, and terror.

"Right now, I want to have some fun with you. While using your body, I saw what was in your head. I know what scares you, Cain, that fear embedded in the back of your mind since childhood. About what lives under your bed. And what would happen if it snatched you under the bed with it."

My skin felt clammy and my whole body trembled at Sarah's words. Please don't say it, I pleaded silently. She radiated malevolence, shrouded by pure evil, not a trace of humanity left. "I'm going to make your nightmares come true."

Curling into a fetal position and surrendering seemed the easiest thing to do, but my survival instincts were stronger, shattering the grip of terror paralyzing my mind. I rolled to my side in an attempt to get my legs under me and run, but Sarah's reflexes were like lightning. Her hand clamped around my ankle with the strength of a vise and although I kicked out, her grip never loosened. She began creeping backwards toward the bed, dragging me with her. I knew she was drawing it out to heighten my fear, because she'd already demonstrated her ability to move inhumanly fast.

My hands clawed for something to provide leverage and slow her progress. When my arm brushed against the dresser leg, I arched back, clamping both hands around it. Sarah never let up and my body felt like it might split in half, but she was too strong, and the dresser pulled away from the wall, forcing me to let go.

Sarah was halfway under the bed now, and I had only inches before following her. Out of sheer desperation, I clutched the nightstand, but it tilted, overturning the lamp and it fell to the floor, shattering the recently replaced bulb. Now only the flickering light of the television illuminated the room, casting Sarah's face in a shifting array of shadows. I fought against the impulse to scream, afraid it would bring Mom or Maddie to my room, and knowing I'd rather endure whatever Sarah had planned for me than put them in danger. Nothing was left to hold onto, and I focused on the peaceful nighttime sky outside my window, knowing it might be the last thing I ever saw.

Being under the bed, alone in near total darkness with something that was no longer alive had been the leading cause of my sleepless nights as a child. When I was eight years old, Mom had been watching *The Shining*. I'd wanted to watch it also, pleading with her I was old enough and wouldn't have bad dreams. Some of my favorite books were from R.L. Stine's *Goosebumps Series*, so how could the movie be any worse than that? She'd chuckled and promised me we'd watch it together when I was a teenager, then tucked me in bed. Confident that I knew best, I'd gotten up, slithered behind the couch, and peeked around the corner at the television. What I'd seen had haunted my nightmares for many months after. It was the part where Danny went in room 237 and saw the lady in the bathtub. On those sleepless nights, more often than not, it was her rotting corpse pulling me under the bed.

Sarah wasn't as old and decayed as the bathtub lady, but she didn't look much better, and all those wakeful nights I'd spent huddled under my covers in terror, eyes tightly shut, washed over me and I felt myself withdrawing, seeking a safe place in my mind. The thundering sound of my quick, raspy breathing surrounded us, but I couldn't calm myself. Like when I was a child, my eyes were squeezed shut and if I looked at Sarah, I'd become unhinged and never make it back.

"Look at me, Cain," Sarah hissed. Her breath was fetid, smelling of rotten meat and dank earth and I instinctively turned away. Grabbing my chin, Sarah jerked my head back to face her. "I said look at me! What happened to the man who laughed at all those horror movies? You yelled at the screen, mocking those characters and telling them how stupid they were. Did you piss your pants yet, Cain? You're pathetic," she scoffed, shaking me so hard that my head snapped back. "Open your eyes!"

Tremors wracked my body and I knew there was no escaping her. When she was alive, Sarah had been roughly five and a half feet tall, around 120 to 130 pounds and I could have easily shaken her off, but this Sarah had the strength of ten men and her hands were like steel clamps as she gripped my upper arms. I knew I had to look at her. If I didn't, she'd keep tormenting me.

Maybe if I gave her what she wanted, she'd grow tired of this game and leave. I needed to rip off the band-aid and get it over with.

Knowing the light from the television would be diminished by the blankets hanging over the side of my bed and partially mask Sarah's features gave me the extra push needed. My lids shot open and I was confronted with a demon who delighted in my intense terror.

"W-what do you want, Sarah? Just do whatever it is and g-get it over with and leave." My teeth were chattering so much, it was difficult to speak clearly.

"Not so fast, Cain. Just because I'm dead doesn't mean I can't have some fun, right?" The putrid smell of her breath as it wafted across my face made my stomach churn. "You were right before, you know. I'd been with Nathan and we had a real heart to heart conversation, baring our souls to each other. He was coming to see you, to lead you to my grave, but I couldn't let that happen.

"I hid in his car while he drove here, waiting for the right moment to surprise him. I knew if any of the three admitted what they'd done to me, it would be Nathan. He and Liam were like dogs trailing after Jacob, obeying him, seeking his approval. But Nathan had always hung back a little, even questioned Jacob a couple of times, and I knew he wasn't as cruel as the other two."

"Then why did you hurt him?" I asked, barely whispering.

"Because he hurt me!" Sarah screeched, her hands clutching my upper arms even tighter, spittle spraying my face. "He helped hold me down while Jacob ripped my shirt! If Nathan hadn't been trying so hard to please Jacob, maybe he would have seen how wrong he was and helped me instead!"

"Sarah, what they did to you – it never should have happened, and they deserve to be held responsible, but not like this, you can't kill them. It's wrong." Through the pale rays of light, I saw her brows furrow, and her grip on my arms loosened slightly. A part of me, a very small, skeptical part, because I knew Sarah, wondered if my words were having an effect on her.

My brief moment of hope was shattered when her face morphed back into the murderous demon who only accepted excruciatingly painful blood sacrifice as payment for the wrongs done to her.

She moved closer, one hand releasing my upper arm, moving slowly up to my shoulder, then to the back of my neck, her decomposing hand running through my hair. Her other hand trailed up my arm, then to my face, and gently stroked my cheek before clamping the back of my neck, holding me in place.

The quivering began at my core, then jumped to my limbs, my muscles twitching and seizing, I was so repulsed and horrified by Sarah's touch. Instinctively, I jerked away, but the hand clutching the nape of my neck might as well have been made of titanium.

"How does this make you feel, Cain? I know you're straining to pull away from me, your body aching to be free. You're being held against your will and there's nothing you can do about it. What if I do this?" She inched closer, touching her forehead to my own as her arms encircled me, drawing me against her rotting form.

Chaos controlled my body and mind. Physically, I felt like a trapped animal, desperate to put some distance between us and escape the abomination wrapping her body around mine. Psychologically, I was in panic mode, my worst nightmare multiplied exponentially, damaging me forever. This wasn't really happening. I was asleep and needed to wake up, or close my eyes and Sarah would be gone when I opened them.

"How do you like this, Cain?" she hissed. "Do you like being forced to do something you clearly don't want to do? Do you like having my arms around you? Being this close to me?" My head shook violently, but I was unable to speak. "Neither did Nathan. He was babbling like a lunatic, begging me to let him go, not to hurt him. But that wasn't going to happen, not after he helped hold me down for Jacob."

Sarah was so close her lips grazed my ear and I continued to shudder involuntarily. "I made him go out by the old drive-in, but not so far away that what's left of him wouldn't be discovered. He needs to be found so Jacob knows he's next. I dragged Nathan through the trees, and he screamed all the way, pleading with me. Once he saw the hole in the ground, he knew his fate. After all his crying and begging, killing him was an act of mercy instead of vengeance. He wasn't as fun as Liam and was borderline annoying. But you know what I did before burying him, Cain?"

"N-n-no. I don't want to know. Please, please….just don't tell me."

Sarah backed away far enough to see my face, thrilled at my vulnerability. "Right before pushing the dirt over him, I ripped off his hands – the hands that held me down for Jacob. The hands that wouldn't be able to push the dirt from his face or claw his way to the surface. He was shrieking when the dirt fell over him and I could heard his muffled screams several minutes after." The image of Nathan lying there, bleeding and terrified, stole my breath, making me feel light-headed. Knowing the last minutes of his life were filled with such fear and revulsion – it was too painful and disturbing to think about.

"Since killing Nathan wasn't as enjoyable as I'd hoped, I need something to lighten my mood. And I know just what that is." Sarah moved her hand from the back of my neck and brushed her fingers across my lips.

No. For the love of all that's holy, God in heaven, please, no....not that. Her putrefied mouth stretched obscenely, knowing the thought of her kiss brought only feelings of disgust and terror. My synapses were sending out signals faster than I could process them. Fear, loathing, horror, disbelief, and denial ricocheted through every cell of my being. Run, fight, escape.....I couldn't accept the fact I was defenseless. No, nonononno......

Sarah leaned toward me and as her icy, decaying lips met mine, my mind shut down and I knew nothing else.

CHAPTER 30

My head jerked up, whacking the underside of the bed frame, and I cursed in pain. What was I doing under here? Did I roll out of bed and not feel it? Then, like a storm cloud releasing heavy rain, everything flooded back in a dizzying rush – Sarah dragging me under the bed, telling me how she killed Nathan, and then she'd…. . No. Can't think about that right now. My mind refused to wrap around what I'd experienced – and Sarah's filthy, murdering lips on me.

But I'd survived. For some reason, she'd let me live.

After scrambling out from under the bed, I dashed downstairs. The house was quiet in the early gray dawn hours, so there was no one to see me when I stumbled into the living room and ripped the cushions from the couch, tossing them to the floor. I shoved my hand between the crevices, wriggling my fingers until I felt the leather cord, then yanked out the talisman. After draping it around my neck, I dropped to my knees and kissed the cold metal, knowing I was protected again. I hoped. Last night, I'd thought it was final curtain call for me. Remembering the way Sarah had touched me, I felt contaminated, unclean all over and craved a long, hot shower.

· · · · ·

When Finn picked me up for school that morning, I filled him in on Nathan's death and last night's sordid events. On the way, we stopped off at an old laundromat housing one of the few remaining pay phones in the city, and made an anonymous call to the police department, telling them we'd seen an abandoned car near the drive-in movie theater. Since Nathan's parents had reported him missing, connections were made, bad news traveled faster than Eby at the first whiff of tuna, and by late afternoon, news about Nathan's death and how he'd died was all over school. Rumors and suspicion circulated again.

When Finn and I were leaving soccer practice - I'd finally been cleared to play – we found Jacob pacing in front of Finn's car, glancing back over his shoulder every few seconds. His head snapped up as we neared and he made a beeline for me.

"You seem a little jumpy, Jacob. I almost didn't recognize you with the baseball hat pulled so low over your eyes. If I didn't know better, I'd say you were trying to disguise yourself," Finn said.

"She did this, didn't she? Sarah killed Nathan?" Jacob asked, seizing my forearm, which was covered in Sarah's hand-shaped bruises from the night before. Heat coursed through me and I shook him off, but got in his face, only inches away.

"Yes, Sarah killed him, Jacob. Do you believe us now? Maybe if you hadn't kept Nathan from talking to us, he'd still be alive, we'd have found Sarah's body, and you wouldn't be scared out of your mind. Did you think about that?" Jacob immediately went on the defensive, shoved me, and drew back his fist. In an instant, Finn grabbed Jacob's arm, twisted it behind his back, and shoved him face down to the ground. Jacob grunted in pain and tried to reach Finn, but the way he held Jacob's arm didn't allow for wiggle room.

"Can't you play nice just once, Jacob? Look what you made me do. And you know how I hate violence." Which was absolutely not true. Finn had never shied away from a fight if he was provoked. "Will you stop going after Cain if I release you? Think about it, Jacob. You may want to show more respect to the guy who could save your unessential life."

Jacob stopped struggling and nodded, letting out a huff of breath as Finn freed him.

"Get in the car. We're already drawing enough attention," I said, as our teammates filtered out of the field house, many of them looking in our direction questioningly, wondering if a fight was brewing. A couple of guys moved in our direction, but Finn waved them off.

The three of us got in Finn's car, Jacob in the back and us up front. Although we weren't going anywhere yet, Finn started the car and turned on the air conditioner, because you never sat in a parked car in the Charleston heat without air conditioning if you could help it.

"Why are you here, Jacob? Does this mean you believe us?" I asked.

Jacob's gaze bounced from window to window, continuously checking to see if anyone was around the car, and his hands were in constant motion, raking over his thighs to his knees. He resembled strung out or detoxing junkies I'd seen in movies. "I've never believed in ghosts, they don't exist. You die, and you stay dead. That's the way it works. You don't come back."

Finn rolled his eyes. "So what do you want, Jacob? Why are you here wasting our time?"

Jacob stared at the floor, his hands still for a moment as he clasped them together. "Maybe you're right, okay? I'm not sure what to believe anymore. All I know is, two of my friends were murdered, you say you've seen Sarah, and I'm the only one left. She's the link between us and you know details we've never told anyone."

"So you admit it? The three of you were at my house with her the night she died?"

"We didn't kill her!" Jacob shouted, lunging toward us, his hands slamming against the headrests of our seats. Finn's hand shot out, grabbed the front of Jacob's shirt and shoved him back.

"I warned you once, Jacob. Don't make me come back there." Jacob scowled at Finn and I knew that under different circumstances, a time when Jacob didn't need our help, fists would be flying and I'd be in the middle trying to separate them.

"Alright. You didn't kill Sarah. So what happened, Jacob?"

Jacob slumped in the seat and took a deep breath. "It was a bet between us. Sarah never talked to anyone, didn't have any friends, and definitely never had a boyfriend. It's not that she was bad to look at, but she always acted like she was better than the rest of us, you know, because of her grades. Like we were all stupid or something.

"Liam and Nathan dared me to ask her out, make her think I was interested. They said I couldn't do it, that she'd never go out with me, but I knew I could make her believe me. A girl like that, someone guys don't see even when they're looking directly at her, who gets noticed by someone like me - I had her practically groveling at my feet after a couple of weeks."

Finn snorted. "You ooze modesty, Jacob."

"You know it's true, Finn. Look how fast Erin jumped in my bed," Jacob sneered.

"And you think that's a good thing? She did it because you're such a great guy? Look how fast she'd jump in anyone's bed if it suited her purpose."

"Can the two of you cut it out so we can get on with this? Sarah could show up at any time."

Jacob and Finn were locked on each other, but nodded. Barely.

"I convinced her to come to a party at a house under construction. Told her a lot of people would be there, she'd be my date, and everyone would know we were together, and she agreed to come. Liam and Nathan said that was the last step in making her think I really liked her – getting her to the house."

"My house. The one haunted by Sarah's blood-crazed ghost."

"Yeah. I guess so," Jacob agreed, shifting uncomfortably. "Anyway, when we met up that evening, she looked different, you know? Like she'd put on makeup or something and dressed differently, stuff like the other girls wore. When we got to your house, she mentioned how no one else was there, but we convinced her they were picking up the keg and just running late. I told her we should go up to the attic, said the view was nice and we'd be able to see when the other guys showed up.

"Once we got upstairs, Liam and Nathan changed the stakes. They said I had to kiss her to win the bet, then they laughed about it. Sarah knew then it was all a lie. She spazzed out and started screaming at me, saying she never should have trusted me and was leaving. I explained it was just a joke, no harm no foul, and she didn't have to go foaming at the mouth. Just give me a kiss and I'd win the bet. No big deal."

I'd known Jacob was shallow and only thought about himself, but to treat someone like that, embarrass and attack them, all for a bet? To think so little about another person's feelings? His story varied from Sarah's, but I figured neither was the absolute truth, more somewhere in between.

"Is that the story you're sticking with, Jacob? According to Sarah, there was a little more to it. She said Liam and Nathan held her down."

In response, Jacob raised his chin and halfway smiled, almost as if he was gloating.

"You know, Cain, maybe we should let Sarah have him. After hearing this story, now I'm thinking maybe that's not such a bad thing," Finn said, his voice full of contempt as he glowered at Jacob.

"You might be right."

"How could you treat someone like that, Jacob? Were you raised by a pack of feral dogs?"

Jacob's brows drew together in confusion. "What do you mean? It was just a joke, guys. What's the big deal?"

I shook my head in disbelief. "Just finish the story and get this over with."

Jacob shrugged his shoulders and continued. "Anyway, Sarah didn't want to kiss me. She kept screaming and Liam and Nathan were still laughing, but now the idiots were laughing at me, and I knew they'd never let me live it down, so I grabbed Sarah's shoulders."

"You forced her to kiss you?" I asked.

"I see mug shots written all over your future, Jacob. What's wrong with you? She said *no*. It should have ended there."

"I forgot, you're used to hearing no from girls all the time, Finn, but I'm not. Even if they say no, they're just playing hard to get. Girls think guys like that kind of thing."

Finn dove for the back seat, but I grabbed the back of his collar before he made it over. "Stop! Jacob, just finish the story."

With Jacob breathing heavily and staring daggers at Finn, I knew he was seething, but needed us too much. Finn knew it, too, which is probably why he smirked at Jacob.

"Anyway, she pushed me away before I could kiss her, and it made me mad, you know? No girl has ever shoved me away, but I knew she really wanted me to kiss her, and I told Liam and Nathan to hold her. Sarah kept fighting, trying to get away and her stupid heel must have gotten caught in something, because the next thing we knew, she'd tripped and stumbled backwards and hit her head on the floor. When she stood up, blood was dripping in her eyes and I guess she couldn't see very well. She had on some kind of scarf thing and wiped off the blood, then tried to run, but missed the first step and fell. She screeched all the way down the stairs.

"Then there was silence. I don't know what was worse. Hearing the screaming or the way it cut off when she hit the bottom."

Jacob stared straight ahead, his eyes unfocused as he remembered. He wasn't fooling me – remorse wasn't part of his genetic makeup and I wished him nightmares for the rest of his life. However long that would be. "What happened after that?"

His head snapped up, almost like he was surprised to find us there. "We ran down the stairs to check on Sarah, but she wasn't moving. Her head was still bleeding a little, but the scarf kept it from dripping, and one of her legs was twisted around and I knew it was probably broken. Liam felt for a pulse, but said he couldn't find one. Nathan and I tried CPR, but nothing worked."

"Did you call 911? Call anyone at all for help?" I asked.

Jacob looked incredulous, his brows raised. "Call for help? Do you know how much trouble we would have been in? Besides, it was too late and there was nothing anyone could do, because she was dead."

"So you just gave up on her. Did you ever think about at least dropping her off at the emergency room? You didn't even need to go in with her. All you had to do was get Sarah to someone who could have helped her." It was inconceivable to me Jacob was so self-absorbed that he and his friends getting in trouble outweighed the cost of Sarah's life. They had tricked her into believing Jacob wanted to be with her, lured her out there, and then didn't seek help after she was injured. Don't get me wrong, Sarah's murderous vengeance was unconscionable, but no one deserved what those three had done to her.

"Even if we'd gotten her to a hospital and they'd revived her, she would have told them what we did. Our parents would have killed us and we were trespassing in that house."

"What about her parents? Did you think what it would be like for them? Not ever knowing what had happened to her? The pain and grief they'd go through? Wait, what am I saying? Of course you didn't think about them. You were only worried about saving your own pathetic lives." If I didn't quit running my hands through my hair, I wouldn't have any left, but Jacob was making me crazy. "What else?"

"We knew we couldn't put her in the trunk of our cars, I've seen on television shows about hairs and fibers and all that, so we decided to bury her. Nathan had some camping equipment in his car, so we got a shovel and carried her through the woods until we found a good place. The grave's pretty far from your house and it's well hidden, so you'd never find it without me, Cain. And if you have any ideas about going to the police and telling them what happened, think again. Her body is in the vicinity of your house and you know a lot of details about her disappearance. I'll deny everything. You've been acting so weird at school anyway, it wouldn't be a big stretch to come up with some motive for you killing Liam and Nathan either."

What? Jacob had ideas of pinning this on me? But then I frowned and pulled back. Because Jacob was right. My actions had been out of character lately - stalking football practice more than once, huge public breakup with my ex-girlfriend, who was now dating Jacob, and spouting stories about a vengeful ghost. All circumstantial, but it wouldn't take much for the cops to look in my direction if someone pointed them my way.

Finn had been silent for an abnormal amount of time, and I turned to see his reaction to Jacob's story.

"I'm trying to think of a good reason, just one, to keep from tying you up, wrapping you in a pretty box, and delivering you to Sarah myself. That's after I strip you naked to make it easier for her to get to your protruding body parts. I'll bet she's got something special planned for you, Jacob. Probably saving the most brutal method of killing for last, don't you think?"

The color visibly drained from Jacob's face and his hands trembled as he rubbed his forehead.

"Jacob, you may not have to answer for Sarah's death now, but some day you will, and that's between you and God. If you're even given the chance to explain," Finn said.

Amen to that.

CHAPTER 31

Trudging through the marshy area behind my house with Finn and Jacob, surrounded by menacing darkness, wasn't at the top of the list of things I'd like to do. But if it could help us rid the world of the murdering evil spirit also known as Sarah, I'd dress up as prom queen, wear the biggest sparkly tiara I could find, and sing Zippity-Doo-Dah.

My whole body felt like a warm, damp sponge from the humidity. And then there were the mosquitoes – I'd lost at least a pint of blood. I carried a forty pound bag of salt, unsure of how much we'd need, but I figured the more the better. Finn lugged a container of gasoline, and Jacob a bag of other supplies, leading the way through the woods with a flashlight. All three of us carried shovels. It had been several months since Sarah was buried, so we weren't sure how hard the ground would be at her grave. Since I'd first met Mona and learned which materials were required to get rid of Sarah, I'd stocked all the items in the garage for when we'd need them. Once we found out where she was buried, the last thing I wanted to do was go on a shopping spree.

"Jacob, we've been walking for a while now and I'm beginning to wonder if we're going in circles. Are you sure you remember where Sarah is buried?"

"How could I forget something like that, Finn? It's not like I bury a body every day."

"Well, you lied about the first one, so who's to say it's never happened before? Maybe we should start correlating your whereabouts with the backs of milk cartons."

Jacob stopped and faced Finn, the glow from the flashlight revealing a scowl across Jacob's face. "It wouldn't take much for me to add another grave, Finn, so I'd suggest you shut your face."

"Come on, guys. Lock it up until we get this over with."

"Keep your dog on a leash, Cain, and this will go a lot faster."

Before Finn had a chance to react, I jumped in front of him. "Don't even think about it," I hissed. "Keep the end game in sight, alright? Once Sarah's gone, you can deal with Jacob."

I knew Finn was close to erupting and it was killing him to keep silent, but he nodded and continued.

We'd been walking about twenty minutes and after passing through two more swarms of mosquitoes, Jacob came to a halt and surveyed the area with his flashlight. "We're close. There, behind that grouping of rocks," he said, sweeping the beam over a pile of mossy rocks rising a few feet from the ground. "We thought maybe the rocks would keep the animals from getting to her body," he said, pulling at his collar. At least he had the decency to look guilty after that statement. But since it was Jacob, he was probably just stretching his shirt away from his sticky body.

Jacob led us around to the other side of the rocks and we dropped our equipment, while he took the camping lanterns out of his bag and set them in a semi-circle, allowing us enough light to see what we turned up in the dirt. Although I knew this was what needed to happen to erase Sarah from this world, it still didn't lessen the creep factor of being with an accidental murderer in a sinister forest and digging up the body of his victim, someone who would take great pleasure in gutting me.

"How deep is she buried, Jacob?" I asked.

"Um, maybe a few feet at the most? We were pretty nervous and just wanted to finish it and get away from here."

"Yeah, it was probably still early and you had other parties to get to, right?" Finn voiced exactly what I'd been thinking, but didn't want to waste any time starting a fight with Jacob.

"Look, Finn, I'm willing to forget you said that because I don't want to spend any more time here than I have to. I mean, it's pretty spooky, don't you think? It kind of feels like we're being watched," Jacob said, scouring the perimeter of light given off by the lanterns.

Honestly, I halfway expected Sarah to make an appearance here tonight because I didn't see her going down without a fight. Would she know we were here? Was it something she could sense? Finn and I were wearing our protection amulets and we'd given one to Jacob, but that didn't mean Sarah wouldn't defend her grave and try to prevent us from salting and torching her remains. "Let's just get started."

The three of us dug in silence for a period of time, but when we didn't turn up anything, Jacob admitted he might be off a few feet, so we split up to cover a broader area. We'd trekked through a marshy area to get here, but now we were on solid ground and without any rain over the past few weeks, the digging was strenuous and all three of us were dripping sweat and dirt.

For a while, the only noises we heard were shovels hitting the packed earth, a few curses here and there, and the occasional slap of a hand against mosquitoes feeding on exposed body parts.

"I've got something," Finn said, his voice wavering a little. "Bring over a light."

Jacob grabbed a lantern and we rushed over to where Finn had been digging. About two feet down, there was what looked like part of a yellow purse. "This is it," Jacob said, swallowing loudly. "We wrapped her body in an old blanket and almost forgot her purse. Liam threw it in while we covered her up."

The three of us continued digging, but a little more carefully now that we knew Sarah's body was there, because we didn't want to stab her with a shovel. Despite all the unspeakable things she'd done, it still seemed disrespectful. A few more inches down, we were hit by a wall of stench, the smell of a rotting, decaying body. The blanket they'd used had done nothing to contain that pungent odor and we all lunged away from the grave, seeking fresh air. Jacob gagged and turned to vomit into a bush.

"Breathe through your mouth," Finn said. "It makes it a little easier to handle." The thought of that smell in my mouth was enough to make me look for a bush of my own, but at least the odor wasn't quite as overwhelming.

"Does the salt have to be directly on her body or can it be poured onto the blanket?" Finn asked.

That thought hadn't occurred to me until Finn mentioned it, but I didn't want to take any chances. "Just to be sure, let's sprinkle it directly on her body. We'll have to dig around her to remove it."

We shoveled a little more, brushing dirt away from the blanket, until my hand hit something that didn't feel like dirt or a blanket and I jerked away in revulsion, afraid of what I'd just touched. "Everyone stop. Don't uncover any more. Finn, bring the light closer," I said, my voice unsteady.

My fears were confirmed when the lantern revealed a gruesome sight. Sarah's hand had either fallen out of the blanket or she'd worked it free, and dirt was encrusted under her jagged and broken fingernails. Small patches of skin were missing, which I assumed were from insects or whatever was in the ground with her.

Jacob's eyes bulged, and his mouth opened and closed as he struggled to find words.

"Sarah wasn't lying, Jacob. She really was alive when the three of you dumped her body. How could you have been so careless?" Finn asked, his voice growing in intensity as he accused Jacob.

"W-w-w-we thought she was dead! Liam checked for a pulse! He said she was dead!"

"And none of you idiots thought to confirm it? Were you dropped on your head as a child or just born this stupid?" Finn was unable to stand still, pacing and muttering to himself in his anger.

Jacob shook his head rapidly as he continued staring at Sarah's exposed hand, unable to accept the abominable result of his egotistical actions, which was now lying in a decomposing pile in front of him. "He's right, Jacob. Why wouldn't you and Nathan have confirmed what Liam said? This was a person's life and you treated her no better than trash you toss to the curb."

"You murdered her!" Finn yelled, his voice gruff and coarse with outrage. "Maybe you didn't mean to, I really don't care, but your asinine bet and misguided belief that all women want you got her out here and then got her killed! How can you live with yourself, Jacob? Really - I want to know."

Even though I felt the same emotions as Finn, I knew it wouldn't do any good for both of us to attack Jacob. But how did Jacob go on about his life and sleep at night, knowing what they'd done to Sarah? If I'd been in the same situation, I would have called for help right away, no matter the consequences, because the truth would come out eventually and hiding it would only make matters worse. And Sarah would still be alive. I liked to think I was a good person and not stupid enough to play puppet master with someone else's life over a moronic bet.

Jacob set his sights on Finn, his mouth drawn in a hard line, jaw squared, the shock of burying Sarah alive having worn off as his self-defense mode activated. "Look, I told you it was an accident and we believed Sarah was dead when we buried her. We thought there was nothing we could do for her, so calling for help wouldn't have helped anyone. Our lives would have been ruined over something we didn't mean to happen and it's not fair to punish us for it, so just shut up about it and let's get to the reason we came here."

Again I thought maybe it wouldn't be such a bad thing to let Sarah have a few minutes alone with Jacob before we salted and burned her body. He was both directly and indirectly responsible for all of this - Sarah's death, the haunting and killing - and he only cared about how it could have affected him. His lack of compassion sickened me and I almost felt sorry for him. Almost.

"What about Sarah's parents, Jacob? Going through life and never knowing if their daughter was alive or dead? At least give them some closure and take responsibility. It's called being an adult and accepting the consequences of your actions," I said, knowing my words would have little, if any effect on Jacob. He was incapable of seeing the big picture and only worried about the impact on his own little world.

"If you're so worried about Sarah's parents and their feelings, why didn't you go to them when you began seeing her, Cain? Don't judge me until you take a look at yourself."

Jacob's words stunned me into silence. I'd thought about seeing them when I believed Sarah was here to get a message to her parents, not for vengeance. Outside of that, no, it had never occurred to me to go to Sarah's parents. What would I have told them? The ghost of your daughter is a psychopathic killer with a taste for blood? Don't count on seeing her in your afterlife? No matter what Sarah had become, hearing revelations like that about their daughter, assuming they'd even believe me, could only hurt them more, not help.

"We could stand here all night discussing Jacob's lack of humanity and intelligence, and he'd still be dumber than a brick, so can we just do this?" Finn asked, ripping the top off the bag of salt.

Finn and Jacob were like cats hissing at each other every few minutes, but worked silently as Jacob gently pushed the blanket away from the rest of Sarah's body, a sight that would headline my nightmares for years to come, while Finn dumped the forty pound bag of salt into the grave, spreading it over Sarah's body and making sure she was thoroughly covered. I poured a generous amount of gasoline over the salt, then pulled out the box of matches I'd taken from the kitchen. Before striking it against the side of the box, I felt the urge to say a prayer, not only to ask forgiveness for the irreverent act we were about to perform, but to request that it be successful and eradicate Sarah from our lives so she could move on – to wherever her soul deserved to go. I'd leave that decision to someone else, but if it were up to me, Sarah would be descending instead of ascending.

I struck the match, the smell of sulfur permeating the night air. The flame wavered a bit in the soft breeze and I took a deep breath, the gravity of the situation weighing heavily upon me, before tossing the match into Sarah's shallow grave. The blaze caught immediately and the three of us watched as the fire danced in the darkness, throwing a medley of shapes on the surrounding trees.

Maybe it was my imagination or just wishful thinking, but I thought I heard an agonizing scream in the distance, and my head shot in that direction. Finn turned in slow circles, probing the shadows for a threat, readying himself. "You heard it too?"

In the seconds it took Finn to ask that question, the scream grew in intensity as it echoed throughout the nighttime air. It was a cry full of deep anguish and pain and if it had come from someone other than Sarah, I'd be sympathetic.

"She's coming!" I yelled. Before I could say anything else, something slammed into my back, hard enough to knock me forward several steps and close enough to the fire that the smell of singed eyebrows filled my nostrils. If Finn hadn't grabbed the back of my shirt, I'd probably have roasted right along with Sarah.

Her howl of pain had stopped when she hit me, but Jacob was squealing like a banshee, nearly as loudly as Sarah had been. He sounded hysterical and when I turned in his direction, I saw why.

Sarah was floating six feet above the ground directly in front of Jacob, her flashing eyes filled with hate. She resembled Medusa, as ropes of hair danced around her head like snakes. "What's wrong with me?" she hissed. "I'm being ripped apart!"

Jacob had stopped screaming, but was now catatonic, his mouth hanging open and a string of drool dripping past his chin. He swayed back and forth as his hands clawed at his cheeks. Either he'd forgotten about the protection amulet he was wearing or doubted it would work, but either way, he was terrified out of his mind.

"We're releasing you from this realm, sending your soul on to whatever waits for you," I replied, backing away from her. I knew the amulet worked, but separating myself from a raging spirit bent on death and destruction and possibly on a one-way trip to hell seemed like common sense. With a sideways glance to her grave, I noticed there wasn't much left to burn.

A high-pitched keening noise began in the back of Jacob's throat and

Finn's hand cracked across his face in an attempt to force him back to reality. "Jacob, get hold of yourself! She can't touch you while you're wearing the amulet!" Jacob's head snapped to the right as Finn's hand connected with his cheek and he seemed more lucid after that.

"You!" Sarah screeched. "After what you did to me, it should be you burning in that grave, Jacob Headley! I was coming for you tonight and what happened to Liam and Nathan was child's play compared to what was planned for you." Jacob had returned from the edge of insanity, but he hunched over and wrapped his arms around himself in an attempt to make himself smaller and his body quivered violently.

Sarah jerked forcefully from side to side and her head tilted back as a scream erupted from deep inside her and I could see the outline of the trees through her fading form. It was working, I thought, ready to collapse at the relief that coursed through me. Mona had been right. Burning Sarah's body, something her spirit was attached to, would cause her to cross over and leave this world.

Sarah was almost imperceptible now, only her facial features still definable and her eyes fiery coals. "I promise you'll never be safe, Jacob!" A fierce wind tore through the canopy of trees, spraying dirt and nearly knocking us off our feet, and then – Sarah was gone. The fire had burned itself out, with only faint tendrils of smoke swirling into the air and disappearing, just as Sarah had.

All the material from Sarah's clothing had burned away, along with any remaining skin, but some solid chunks remained, which I assumed were bits of bone and teeth. It was disheartening to think when all was said and done, those remnants were all that remained of a person. I mean, I'm sure Sarah's parents were left with good memories of her, but she was basically a loner and not very sociable, and had no close friends or siblings. She'd been a good student and maybe some teachers would think of her every now and then, but Sarah hadn't really been here long enough to make an impact, to see where life would have taken her.

"Are we done?" Jacob growled. For someone who probably needed to change his pants judging by his reaction to Sarah, he'd recovered quickly.

"Yeah, I guess we are. Mona didn't mention anything else that needed to be done. Finn and I can throw some dirt over the embers to make sure they're out."

Jacob snatched up the shovel and other things he'd been carrying, then turned to both of us, stabbing his finger at us as he spoke. "This stays between us. Not a word to anyone, you got that? If I even think you've told anyone, I'll deny everything and come after both of you."

"Yeah, because hurting us wouldn't make you look guilty. You know what needs to be done, Jacob, so why don't you just grow a set and do it," Finn said, moving a step closer in Jacob's direction.

"Just back off, Finn. I already told you I'm not ruining my life over some stupid girl that couldn't take a joke, so get out of my way."

Finn looked to me, silently asking if we should handle this right now, but I shook my head very slightly. "Let's just get out of here before someone comes and we have to answer some impossible questions. We'll deal with everything later."

Jacob narrowed his eyes at Finn and strutted by him, slamming his shoulder into Finn's as he passed. Maybe deep down Jacob was more disturbed by tonight's events than he admitted and was just putting on a good front. Maybe once he got to his car, he'd break down in tears over what he, Liam, and Nathan had done to Sarah. Or not. Maybe I was totally misreading him, but somehow I didn't see repentance in his future.

"I think you're wasting your breath trying to get Jacob to confess what happened, Finn. No matter what we say, he'll never believe what he did was wrong. Let's get all this stuff picked up and go home. I plan on sleeping like a normal person tonight instead of waking up every hour because I think Sarah's watching me sleep or waiting to pull me under the bed again."

. . . . .

After Finn and I put away the shovels and other equipment in the garage and he went home, I crept into the house. Mom and Maddie were already in bed and if Mom saw me in this condition, I was too exhausted to lie. I padded up the stairs, then down the hallway to my room, dreading the maelstrom that might be waiting for me. Although I knew I'd seen Sarah depart this world, somewhere deep down I believed it was too good to be true.

The door was closed, so I first put my ear to it and listened, just in case. Silence. Normally, I'd consider that a good sign, but it wouldn't be the first time Sarah had been quiet, coiled and waiting to strike like a cobra.

My hands trembled and I took a deep, calming breath, then cautiously turned the knob and inched the door open. When it creaked loudly, I froze, my knees threatening to buckle, and wondered if the past few weeks spent with Sarah would have me on tranquilizers for the rest of my life.

But I was greeted with my normal, chaotic-looking bedroom. Nothing seemed out of the ordinary. Just as I was about to step over the threshold, Eby came tearing down the hallway, leaped in front of me, landed on a magazine and skidded a few feet before recovering enough to jump onto the bed. I'd swear he did that stuff on purpose.

"What's your problem, Eby?" I loud whispered. "Are you deliberately trying to send me into cardiac arrest?" Being a typical cat, Eby gave me an indignant look, lifted his leg, and proceeded to wash areas that turned my stomach.

Then it hit me. If Eby was in my room, then Sarah wasn't – and I thought I might cry. Or dance around the room in celebration wearing only my underwear. Maybe she really was gone. In my bathroom, I tossed my grimy, sweaty clothes into the hamper, scrubbed the smell of gasoline and burning corpse off my body, then stood under the water until it ran cold. After brushing my teeth, I collapsed into bed, already deeply asleep in the few seconds it took Eby to curl up beside me.

CHAPTER 32

The alarm on my phone woke me the next morning after seven hours of deep, uninterrupted sleep. I couldn't remember the last time I'd felt this good - hopeful even. Like I'd been treading water with a cinderblock hanging around my neck and had finally been cut loose.

I'd forgotten what the life of a normal seventeen-year-old teenager looked like. I went to school, hung out with my friends in between classes, zoned out in chemistry, ate lunch with Lindsey and Finn, and went to soccer practice after school. It felt like coming home to the smell of freshly baked chocolate chip cookies or sliding into the pair of holey jeans that fit just right, but Mom kept threatening to throw out.

My stress-free week continued and on the third day, getting out of the shower at home after soccer practice, I took off my protection amulet. I held it over the trash can, thinking what a relief it would be to get rid of something attached to such bad memories, but then a gut-wrenching thought stopped me.

If Sarah was able to take over my body and murder people, what's to keep another spirit from showing up and threatening me? I mean, who knew what stories Sarah was spreading around wherever she'd wound up? Was there a network of evil spirits that shared information about their hauntings? Did they trade around victims for fun? It might sound like a ridiculous thought, but if someone had told me a few weeks ago what I was getting ready to experience, I would have passed them off as certifiably insane or at least off their meds. Maybe I was also a little paranoid.

Keeping the amulet wasn't such a bad idea after all. Even if I never needed it again, it would be an interesting story to tell my grandkids someday. Or maybe I could sell it on ebay if I was ever short on cash. Knowing what I did now, there could be high demand for a good protection amulet. Opening the top drawer of my desk, I dropped the talisman in where it joined various pencils, hair bands, and loose coins.

. . . . .

Saturday morning dawned clear, with a light breeze and low humidity – a perfect day for a soccer game. I'd already missed four games due to my head injury, so I was anxious to get back on the field today. Finn had picked me up and we'd fallen into our usual pregame routine, getting there early so the two of us could have the field to ourselves for a while.

Thirty minutes later, other team members began straggling in, but instead of joining us on the field, they were huddled up talking animatedly, arms flying about and heads bobbing. If coach noticed they weren't out here warming up, he'd start yelling and bench some of them for the game. Then I saw coach on the sidelines, waving Finn and me over.

"Alright gentleman, everyone have a seat and quiet down," coach said, still trying to herd some guys to the benches.

"Judging by all the conversing going on instead of warming up, I'm guessing you've all heard about Jacob Headley. There are a lot of rumors going around right now, nothing is confirmed, but however it happened, it's a tragedy and our thoughts and prayers are with his family. However, we need to put this aside right now because we have a game to focus on, so I want to see all of you out there on the field, not clustered up speculating on what happened to Jacob."

Was it possible for a person to be alive when their heart stopped? My body was like a block of ice. I guess that's what happened when your heart quit pumping blood.

"Cain?" Finn managed to choke out.

I stopped Riley, one of the players I'd seen whispering with the others earlier. "Riley, what happened to Jacob?"

"You guys didn't hear? His parents found him this morning out by their pool. He was dead."

"How do you know this?" Finn asked, grabbing Riley's upper arm.

"Geez, Finn, lay off the arm," Riley said, shaking him off. "I got the info from my friend, Matt. His dad's a cop and Matt overheard him on the phone. I guess it was a pretty gruesome site, with a lot of blood, but he doesn't know exactly how he died. Judging by his dad's reaction, he said it was pretty nasty."

Finn and I stared at each other in disbelief as Riley jogged onto the field, both of us knowing the truth about what had happened to Jacob, but neither wanting to accept it.

"She's still here," I mostly whispered. "She tricked us somehow."

Finn nodded. "She'll come for us next. She's probably waiting at your house."

Then a weight crashed into me as I realized what that meant. "Mom and Maddie." Finn vaulted over two benches to grab his gym bag with the car keys inside, yelling to coach something about a family emergency, but I was already sprinting towards his car.

I nearly collided with Lindsey in the parking lot. "Cain, did you hear about Ja…"

"We did and we're headed to my house – Mom and Maddie are alone," I said breathlessly.

"I want to come with you."

"No, please no, Lindsey," I said, taking her hands in mine. "I couldn't stand it if something happened to you….it would be my fault and I couldn't live with that."

"We've got to go, Cain!" Finn yelled.

She looked up at me, eyes glistening. "Be careful."

"I promise," I said, wrapping my arms around her, tucking her head under my chin and breathing her in before pulling away. "My cell phone – I left it in my gym b..," but before I could finish the sentence, Finn tossed my bag to me, having picked it up beside his own before running to the car. We both dove through the doors the second they were unlocked, and Finn's tires squealed in protest as he sped out of the parking place before I could close my door.

I frantically dialed Mom's cell phone, begging her to answer, but kept getting her voice mail. Really? Of all the times to not answer her phone. I knew she habitually charged it every night. She'd always said that as a single parent with no other family around, especially the parent of a teenage boy who drove, she couldn't afford to have a dead battery in case something bad happened.

And now something bad might have happened, or possibly be happening soon, and she wasn't picking up. Or maybe she was being prevented from answering it. After the fifth try with no response, I left a message for her to take Maddie and get out of the house as soon as possible and then call me.

Finn weaved in and out of traffic, honking his horn at slow drivers who refused to move to the other lane. "How could she come back, Finn? We did everything Mona told us to do, so why didn't it work!"

"Call her. Call Mona right now and tell her what happened. Maybe she knows something or can help us."

My fingers fumbled through the contact list, cursing as I passed her name, then finally located it and hit dial, listening to the ringing on her end. Just when I was sure it would roll over to voice mail, she answered. "Cain?"

Hearing her voice filled me with confidence. If anyone could help us, it was Mona. "She's back. Sarah is back and she killed Jacob and now she's..."

"Cain, slow down. Lindsey said Sarah was gone, that you'd salted and burned her remains like we discussed."

"We did. We did everything like you instructed and thought she was gone, because I haven't seen her all week, but I guess she was just waiting it out, trying to fool us." I sounded like a babbling idiot, but the words just spilled out. "Finn and I just found out the last of the three guys is dead. They found him this morning."

"Is there any chance it could be a coincidence?"

My shoulder slammed against the door as Finn took a corner on what might had been only two wheels. "I don't see how it could be. We don't have all the details, but from what we heard, it was pretty bloody and terrible." Mona was silent and I worried I'd lost the connection or she'd abandoned us. "Mona? Are you there?" I asked frantically.

"I'm here, Cain, I was just thinking. Where are you now?"

"Finn and I are on the way to my house, if he doesn't get us killed in traffic first. We're afraid Sarah's got my Mom and sister." As I said the words, Finn dodged a car who pulled out in front of us.

"When you burned Sarah's remains, was she there?"

"Yeah – she showed up when the fire began and threatened all of us, screamed like she was in pain, then disappeared."

"Okay. I may know what happened. Either Sarah was never attached to her body in the grave, or she was able to bind herself to something else before being burned."

"What? She could do that? You didn't mention that before." The lightness of the past few days of Sarah-free life faded with a whimper as Mona confirmed that Sarah could, in fact, still be here.

"It's been known to happen, but the odds of it were so low, it never occurred to me it might be a possibility and for that, I'm so very sorry."

"What else would she have attached herself to? One of us that was there? Do you think she's using me again?"

"Are you missing time or having unexplained behavior?"

"No, everything's been normal this week, just like it used to be."

"If you salted and burned the remains in her grave and none of you has experienced blackouts or lost time, then I think Sarah is attached to the place involved in her death. Your house."

CHAPTER 33

I couldn't have heard Mona right. With Finn's loud swearing and the near constant blowing of the car horn, my hearing must have been impaired. "I'm sorry, Mona, what did you say? I don't think I heard you right."

"Your house, honey. I think Sarah has attached herself to your house. It's where she's spent most of her time since she died and where she found you, the person who enabled her to have access to the boys who killed her."

"You want me to burn down my house?" At those words, Finn's head jerked in my direction. Considering how fast the images blurred outside the car window, taking his eyes off the road probably wasn't the brightest idea, but he was as shocked as I was.

"I know it's a drastic measure, Cain, but Sarah is a strong spirit. After taking over your body and killing those boys, she's only grown more powerful. From your description, I'm almost certain she was originally attached to her body, but was able to break that bond and bind herself to the house in order to remain in this plane. It's rare to do something this extreme, but burning your house might be the only thing left to eliminate Sarah."

Although Mona's words made sense in the worst way, burning down our home, besides being nearly impossible to wrap my head around, was an extreme measure. I had no idea if we'd even be able to save anything in the house, like pictures of my Dad, things he'd left us. Mom uploaded all her pictures now, but she still had the actual photos of Maddie and me when we were younger, not to mention the early pictures of her and my Dad. She might never forgive me for what I was about to do. I might never forgive myself, but would do whatever was required to keep us safe. And alive.

"Will you come to help us?" I pleaded.

"I'm already in the car and on my way and I have something that may help. Be careful, Cain, and don't let your guard down. Try to keep Sarah from figuring out what you plan to do. Are you still wearing your protection charm?"

My stomach twisted and I thought about how just a few days earlier I'd been confident Sarah was gone, taken off the talisman, and dropped it in my drawer. "No. I took it off and it's in my bedroom."

"Listen to me, honey. It's crucial that you get to it quickly once you're home. Do you understand?"

"Yeah, I do. Thanks, Mona. You have no idea how grateful I am you're meeting us there."

"Just be careful and trust your instincts, Cain. I'll see you soon." Then she hung up.

"If you're talking about the protection amulet, I have mine in my gym bag. I've still been wearing it, but had to take it off for the game today. You take it."

"No. No way, Finn. You keep it and get Mom and Maddie out. I'll hold off Sarah long enough to make it to my room and get my own. Maybe Mona will be here by then."

"Fine," he huffed. "I'll get them out, but I'm coming back in to help you. I'm not leaving you by yourself with Sarah, dude. You know what she can do."

After what seemed like hours, we turned down my street, Finn's tires screeching as he rounded the corner, then leaving trails of rubber as he slid into my driveway. I leapt from the car, not bothering to close the door, only focused on getting to my family. Finn and I nearly stumbled over each other as we burst through the laundry room, and emerged into the kitchen to see.....Maddie slinging her backpack over her shoulder and Mom wearing her baseball hat, carrying her purse and car keys, headed toward the garage door we'd just come through.

"Boys? What are you doing here? Doesn't the game start soon? Maddie and I were just leaving. Hey, have you seen my phone?"

Adrenaline coursed through my veins and my pulse raced faster than Finn's car. "Where is she? Is she here? Has she hurt you?" I asked breathlessly.

"Is who here, Cain?" Mom asked, her forehead creased in confusion. "What's going on and why aren't you at the soccer game? Finn?"

Just when I began to wonder if I'd jumped to the wrong conclusion about Sarah being here, several things happened at once. First, every cabinet door in the kitchen flew open, expelling their contents with deafening, ear-splitting cracks. With my nerves on edge already, at the sound of the first crack, I shoved Mom to the floor and shielded her with my body, while Finn did the same with Maddie, both of us ignoring their screams of protest. Although all had been calm outside when Finn and I arrived moments earlier, the windows shot open and wind roared through the room, upending chairs, books, plants and pictures, clearing all horizontal surfaces.

Raising my head slightly, I peeked over Mom's head, the force of the wind nearly bringing tears to my eyes. My peripheral vision tracked something moving rapidly up and to my right. I shifted my gaze and what I saw filled me with fear beyond anything I'd felt so far. Sarah crawled along the ceiling directly towards us, her mouth a gaping maw of black, dark eyes incendiary and gleaming in triumph.

"Finn!" I shouted, but he was already watching her as he stood, scooping Maddie into his arms. "Get them both out of here!"

Mom followed our gazes and when she saw Sarah, her eyes widened in disbelief and fright, as her hand covered her mouth to keep from screaming and upsetting Maddie any more than she already was. Finn had tucked Maddie's head against his shoulder so she couldn't see Sarah, something for which I'd be eternally grateful, but she called for me, her arms outstretched as Finn carried her away. "Cain! I want to stay with you, please!"

"Maddie, go with Finn, I'll be alright, I promise."

"Cain, what is that? What's happening? I'm not leaving you here alone!"

"Mom, go, run! You have to go now!" Finn's hands were full with Maddie, so I had to push Mom out the door while she fought to stay behind with me. "Take them somewhere safe, Finn, anywhere but here." With Mom still screaming for me to come with them, I slammed the door and locked it behind her, then turned to face Sarah.

"Where's your protection amulet now, Cain?"

CHAPTER 34

Before I could react, Sarah, floating a couple of feet above my head, grabbed me by the throat, her hand icy and reeking of rot and she looked and smelled as if she'd been in the ground for months. I tried to speak, but her grip was like a vise crushing my windpipe.

"Sacrificing yourself for your precious family, Cain?" she hissed. "If you're wondering why I didn't hurt them before you got here, let's just say I'm feeling kind of generous after what I did to Jacob. Turns out vengeance puts me in better mood. Besides, I knew you'd come running after you heard what happened to him."

Sarah let up on my throat enough for me to speak. "What did you do to Jacob?" I asked, my voice already raspy.

What was left of her mouth stretched into a macabre smile and it chilled me to my core. "I've been looking forward to sharing all the details. You know, even though I'd wanted Jacob dead sooner, the actual experience of it might have been worth waiting for." And that statement chilled me down to my bone marrow. "Let's go somewhere and talk about it."

Sarah jerked me closer to her, again clutching my throat, then we were sailing into the two story family room, as my feet kicked to find purchase to support my weight, hands clawing at Sarah's arms in vain attempts to free myself. All the while I struggled, I heard her gritty, guttural laughs at my useless endeavors. Just when my vision started to blacken around the edges, Sarah slammed me to the floor, my back screaming in protest at the hardwood floors underneath while my lungs gulped in sweet oxygen. As she straddled my upper thighs, she removed her hands from my neck, pinning my shoulders instead. I was trapped, pure and simple, and the likelihood of me retrieving the protection amulet in my bedroom was less than zero. And that was my only chance of staying alive until Mona got here. Assuming Mona could even help.

"Are you comfortable, Cain? No? Well, this is probably as comfortable as you'll be before I kill you, so enjoy it while I tell you about Jacob and his glorious death. Just keep in mind, while you're lying there listening to the details, I want you to know yours will be even more painful, after what you tried to do to me. Burning my body, Cain? Did you really think I wouldn't be able to attach to something else?" As she spoke, black, oozy liquid dripped from her mouth and over her chin, making me want to retch.

"Anyway, we'll deal with that later. Did you enjoy the few nights of peace I gave you? It gave me time to plan Jacob's death. Last night, after he kicked a girl out of his car for not sleeping with him on the first date....oh, wait, it wasn't really a date. He's cheating on Erin, you know, but I can't really blame him for that, and this was just the girl he's sneaking around with.

"When Jacob got home, his parents were out for the evening, so he grabbed a beer and went outside to lie in a lounge chair by the pool. One beer turned into a couple more, and I decided it was time. He was nearly asleep, but when he heard water dripping as I crept out of the pool, he opened his eyes. There was no one there except me to hear his howls of terror, and seeing the effect I had on him, making him experience mind-numbing fear, gave me such a feeling of satisfaction. Can you understand that, Cain?"

"Watching another person literally be scared to death? No, Sarah, I can't understand how that would make you happy," I croaked. It was difficult to talk, partly because she was sitting on me, but also because I was trying not to breathe in her stench.

"Oh, I didn't scare him to death, Cain. No way would I have let him go that easily." Her eyes glittered from the memory of torturing Jacob before she'd killed him. He'd been a narcissistic, loathsome person, but he hadn't deserved persecution. Not to that extent anyway.

"He was blabbering, begging me not to hurt him and apologized for everything they'd done to me. I crawled onto the lounge chair and straddled him, and he was in almost the same position you are now. Jacob tried scooting away, but there was nowhere to go, and I held him in place while he whimpered and pleaded with me.

"I told him how it had felt, regaining consciousness in the dirt, in my shallow grave, not knowing where I was or what had happened. I tried moving, but the blanket wrapped around me bound my arms and legs. Imagine being claustrophobic, Cain, held immobile and unable to breathe. I panicked and struggled to free myself, but that used up what little oxygen I

177

had. It was my own personal hell."

To each his own personal hell. I'd been living through my own since the day I'd met Sarah and the embodiment of my suffering sat astride my chest dragging out the last moments before ending my life.

"I tried to scream, but the weight of the dirt pushed the blanket into my mouth and I knew my time was limited. I managed to free one of my hands and clawed at the dirt, trying to dig myself out or just make a hole to breathe, but I knew it was useless. Just before drawing my last breath, I vowed to come back somehow, to make them feel everything I'd felt. They would know their lives were ending, there was nothing they could do to save themselves, and no one was coming to help them. I'd make sure they died suffering, terrified, and alone in a monstrous, painful way.

"I reminded Jacob how he'd tried to kiss me when the four of us had been in the attic and how angry he'd been when I'd pulled away. I told him I'd changed my mind, and even though Liam and Nathan were no longer here to see it, at least Jacob would know he'd won the bet. When he realized he was about to die and would finally be able to kiss me, it must have broken his mind, judging by the way his body convulsed and the vacant look in his eyes."

After living through the experience of having Sarah kiss me, but mercifully passing out before it happened, I could sympathize with Jacob. I hoped he'd been able to find a room inside his mind, someplace where he could close the door and pretend he was somewhere else. If I hadn't passed out, I would have found a room in my own mind, locked the door and thrown away the key.

"I took his face between my hands to hold him in place and pressed my lips against his. Other than you, Cain, Jacob's the only boy I've ever kissed, and at least he was semi-conscious. He was making a keening, whimpering kind of noise and when I pulled away from him, his eyes had rolled back in his head. I wanted him aware and present, to experience what was happening to him, so I slapped him across the face, hard enough to rock his head to the side, but it seemed to work.

"When Jacob looked at me again, his eyes were more focused, but his body still trembled. I told him in exchange for giving me hope that a guy could genuinely be interested in me, making me believe I'd been enough, then destroying my life and my future, he owed me his heart – literally. Then, just as he comprehended the meaning of that statement, I reached through his chest and ripped out his still beating heart."

Oh no, no, no, no. A roaring began in my ears, blocking all other sound, even my own grating breaths. It was beyond my mental capacity to comprehend what Jacob's last moments had been like. I hoped he'd been unaware of what was happening to him, that his mind had drawn the blinds and closed up shop. Hopefully the alcohol had numbed him somewhat, but I feared seeing Sarah had shocked him sober.

"Stay with me, Cain!" Sarah shouted, as her hand collided with my cheek. "You know, I think after I tore his heart from his body, Jacob was still alive for a few seconds. Do you think that's even possible? He gasped, maybe even tried to say something, but then his head fell back against the chair, his eyes still open even in death, frozen and staring at me. Knowing I was the last thing he saw gave me some peace – but just a sliver.

"I thought once Jacob was taken care of, I'd move on to wherever I go from here, but now I feel the need to take care of some loose ends – that would be you and Finn – and I've been having so much fun being with you, I think I'll hang around a little longer. When you bore me, I'll asphyxiate, disembowel, behead, or exsanguinate you – I haven't decided which. I may even visit that snob ex-girlfriend of yours, considering she was one of the girls who used to laugh and point when I walked through the halls. But no worries. We have plenty of time to figure it out. Unless I decide to…"

Sarah's words were abruptly cut off by a black iron fireplace poker exploding through the front of her chest. And then she disappeared. What. Just. Happened?

CHAPTER 35

"Cain, get up, we don't have much time! Finn, you can come in!"

Mona stood over me, the afternoon sun reflected off her unruly copper curls resembling a halo hugging the back of her head. "Mona? How did you…? What…?"

Finn burst through the kitchen and rushed to the front door, hanging something on the door handle. He then ran to the windows and, with a black marker, began drawing some sort of symbol on the glass.

Mona pulled at my arm, getting my attention. "Run, Cain, get your protection amulet! Sarah will only be gone for a few minutes and we have to get the protection symbol over all the doors and windows."

My head was full of questions, but with the urgency of the situation, I decided answers could wait, and took the steps two at a time, then dashed down the hallway to my bedroom. As soon as I entered, Eby scurried out from under the bed, jumped on the dresser and yowled loudly. He must have been petrified.

I tugged open the desk drawer, fumbling through the pencils, papers, and other clutter before my hand closed around the coolness of the metal amulet. As far as I was concerned, it was the Holy Grail. As I draped it around my neck, Finn sprinted into the room and began sketching the same symbol on my windows. He tossed me a handful of the pendants he'd hung on the doors downstairs.

"Hang these on all of the doors," he said, breathing heavily. "I still have to go up to the attic and draw the protection sigils on that window."

Grabbing Eby, I put him into the bathroom, closed the door, and then hung an amulet over the doorknob. He should be safe there. "Mom and Maddie?" I asked, following him up the attic stairs.

"Your Mom refused to leave without you. It was all I could do to keep her from coming back into the house, but convinced her to stay in the car with

Maddie. Told her help was on the way and I promised to get you out. Besides, I figured Mona would need…."

Before he could finish his sentence, Finn sailed across the attic, yelling as he flew through the air, his fall broken by a stack of boxes.

"Finn! Are you…" But my words were cut off as I felt a tug around my chest, then my back slammed into the window and shattered it, my eyes squeezed together in pain as glass shards splintered my skin. I dropped to the floor where some larger chunks of glass had fallen, incredibly lucky they hadn't sliced into my vital organs instead.

Raising my head, I saw Finn crawling slowly, but at least he was moving. The attic filled with spiteful laughter that seemed to come from every direction, surrounding us and echoing in my mind. If I had even a shred of a chance at surviving this, I knew I'd be haunted by that sound for the rest of my life.

Then my whole body went numb as I realized Sarah had just hurt both of us - while we wore the amulets.

"Sarah, stop!" I called, pulling myself to a standing position. "Leave Finn alone, it's me you want to hurt."

"How is she doing this?" Finn asked, one side of his face already discolored from where he'd hit the boxes or fallen to the floor.

Sarah materialized between us, the iron poker still protruding from her chest. Prying it from herself, she pulled her arm back and launched the poker like a spear at Finn, but he rolled to the side as it narrowly missed him. Guess the effect it had on Sarah had worn off. "Surprised? So am I, but I imagine it's a more pleasant surprise for me than it is for you. I may not be able to touch you, but Jacob's death must have given me that boost I needed to at least push you around a little."

"Cain, she can't stop both of us. You're closest to the door, so get Mona for help." I'd thought about calling to her, but she'd gone to the other side of the house to hang amulets and draw sigils. I doubted she'd even hear me. Sarah would probably knock me unconscious with something if I even tried.

"Yes, Cain, go get Mona. And maybe you'll be pushed down those stairs. I hear it's quite an experience. Try it and I guarantee Finn will be thrown out the window and hit the ground before you reach the bottom of the stairs," Sarah threatened. "I dare you."

I'd never wanted to hurt someone more in my life. If it was remotely possible, I would have killed Sarah again with my bare hands and suffered no regret. We were trapped - our only choices being a gamble that Sarah couldn't kill both of us if I tried to get Mona, or die from being beaten to death, tossed out a window, or suffering a broken neck from falling down the stairs.

But there really wasn't a choice. I wouldn't take chances with Finn's life.

"Well, boys, what should we do first?" While Sarah was busy listing all the ways she'd like to torture us, out of the corner of my eye, I saw Mona reach the top of the stairs, a lit white candle in her hand. Sarah had been too distracted to notice.

Mona began chanting something, drawing closer to Sarah. Sarah stiffened, then swung around to face her. I noticed the pillar candle was engraved with the same sigils Finn had been drawing on the windows.

"Leave this house, spirit. You're not welcome. Depart this realm and cross over to your soul's final destination."

Sarah eyes blazed with a hatred so vast, I sensed it move through the room and wrap around us like a shroud. "You think because you light a candle, wave it in my face, and command me to leave, you can exorcise me? Do you honestly believe it's that easy? Killing another person is nothing to me, you red-headed witch!"

But as Mona continued her chanting, Sarah began to rise and from the look on her face, it wasn't from her own efforts, and there was a flash of uncertainty in her eyes. "What's happening? What have...."

Sarah's mouth continued to open and close, but there was no sound, and although she struggled, she seemed unable to move. Whatever Mona was doing was working.

"I heard the crashes from downstairs and figured she'd shown up again in the attic. Are you guys alright? Are you hurt?"

"Not as much as we would have been if you hadn't gotten here," I said.

"I should have come up here myself. Once I understood how powerful Sarah was, I discussed her with a Wiccan friend, who suggested the sigils in case they were needed. If this works, we won't have to burn the house."

Not burn our home? With the mounting list of things I already had to explain to Mom, not having to rationalize burning down our house lifted a huge burden from my conscience.

"Cain! Cain, are you upstairs?"

No. It couldn't be her. I'd asked her to stay away to keep her safe. Surely she'd listened. "Cain?"

Lindsey was here.

Hearing her niece's voice broke Mona's concentration. That brief lapse was all Sarah needed to free herself from the power that held her.

In that moment, time stood still for me. I saw the sheer joy that broke over Sarah's decomposing face, while Mona's eyes widened in shock, and Finn's features twisted in determination as he shuffled his bruised body in my direction.

I needed to get to Lindsey before Sarah.

"Lindsey, stay where you are! Don't come up here!" Even as the words left my lips, I catapulted myself toward the stairs, taking them three at a time, Finn on my heels. Mona followed us as well, but couldn't keep up.

We sprinted across my room, through the door, and down the hallway toward the stairs, my mind focused only on reaching Lindsey in time, the thought of what Sarah could do to her nearly crippling in intensity.

When Lindsey screamed, it felt like the iron poker had been plunged through my chest instead of Sarah's. "Don't touch her!" I roared.

Finn and I reached the bottom of the stairs to find Sarah on the other side of the family room from Lindsey, but readying herself to attack.

And Lindsey wasn't wearing an amulet.

"Cover her!" I yelled to Finn. He leaped over the back of the couch and threw Lindsey to the floor, shielding her body from Sarah with his own. I charged at Sarah, knowing I couldn't do anything to hurt her, but only hoping for a distraction.

The floor began to rumble and the windows vibrated in their frames, while a gust of wind whipped around us, almost painful in its intensity. With a thundering roar, Sarah shot toward me, passing through my body in an attempt to reach Finn and Lindsey, knowing hurting either of them would be more agonizing to me than any physical torture she exerted.

And then something happened.

Mona reached the living room and held the candle over her head, fixated on Sarah, muttering something I couldn't make out, and moved the candle in a pattern that matched the sigils. Sarah came to a sudden halt only a few feet from Finn and Lindsey, then rose several feet above us.

Her body jerked violently in several directions at once.

"What's happening to me?" Sarah shrieked, as her head snapped back. "It hurts! No! No!" The front door burst inward, slamming against the wall behind it to reveal a dusky, ominous cloud unfurling, winding its way through the room. It snaked around the furniture and rolled between Finn, Lindsey, and me before stopping beside Mona and hovering, as if awaiting her instruction. She raised the candle high and ceased her murmuring. "Remove this spirit from this home, it is unwelcome!"

The cloud collapsed in on itself, building its energy, then erupted toward Sarah and curled around her, pinning her limbs like the blanket she'd been buried with, but was unable to muffle her unearthly wails. In mid scream, Sarah was savagely forced from the house by the hazy mist, her ear-splitting howls echoing in the distance.

And then there was silence.

184

CHAPTER 36

Finn and I explained everything to Mom as best we could and, although skeptical, she'd seen Sarah with her own eyes, and Mona corroborated our story. Of course, she blamed herself and said it was all her fault for buying this house and not listening to me that morning in the kitchen when I questioned her about Sarah. After a few weeks, she was still apologizing every day, even with all my reassurances.

It was difficult to explain how I felt, knowing Sarah was finally gone. I was alive, my family was safe, and there was a profound sense of relief. I was indebted to Mona for everything she'd done.

But I still didn't quite feel like myself, or didn't remember what I'd been like before Sarah had disrupted our lives. I had nightmares in which Sarah would reach deep into my chest and clutch my heart, threatening to rip it from my chest. Sudden loud noises instantly launched me on the defensive, certain someone or something was ready to attack.

Finn diagnosed me as having posttraumatic stress disorder, and maybe it was. Maybe all I needed was time to get over Sarah, live the normal life of a teenager, hang out with friends, and go on dates with Lindsey.

One thing I did know – I had no desire to ever see another horror movie. I'd been the guy who checked out the weird goings on in the attic, and as a result starred in and barely survived my own personal horror flick. It was enough to satisfy my curiosity over several lifetimes and I never wanted to experience it again, on the screen or in real life. There was something to be said for snuggling up on the couch with Lindsey and watching some cheesy rom-coms.

I'd also taken my mattress off the bed frame and put it directly on the floor and started sleeping with a light on. Whatever gets you through the night, right?

EPILOGUE

Sarah had been sure her time in this world was finally over, that she'd been headed straight to an eternity in the underworld. But then she'd caught a glimpse of something others had missed - an important something that would enable her to remain in this house, close to Cain and Finn, biding her time until she could strike. A little girl who was terrified for her brother, someone she loved with all her heart, had ventured away from a worried mother whose attention was diverted by fear for her son's life.

The child had crawled between some bushes under the window by the front door and peeked through the glass. She'd seen horrible, unspeakable things that she hadn't understood, but could never mention to her brother or mother, because she'd disobeyed and broken a promise about staying in the car where she'd be safe.

The little girl had felt nothing when Sarah seized the opportunity before her, but every now and then, the child missed chunks of time and wondered how she'd gotten from one room to another or wound up outside. It was especially scary when she began sleepwalking, always waking at her brother's bedside, gazing down at him while he slept peacefully.

Acknowledgements

The idea for this story was sparked by my cat and loyal furry friend, Shadow. He's crossed the Rainbow Bridge now, but he was a lot like Eby. I've read that black cats are the last to be adopted at animal shelters, but they've been the most loving and personality-oozing pets I've ever had the pleasure of owning. Consider giving them a forever home - you won't regret it.

Thanks to my family – Reese for all your input, suggestions, and encouragement (even though you expect a cut of the profits – and you're assuming there will be any), Tanner for his soccer knowledge, and Mike for pretending to listen (as your eyes glazed over) when I rambled on about this book so many times, but most of all for giving me time to make this dream a reality.

To my parents for being my biggest fans.

From the Writer's Sanctuary – Thanks to Shantele Summa Martin for brainstorming, Rachel Garza for your help and reassurance during a moment of crisis, and C.J. Redwine for your freaking awesome writer's retreats and making me believe this was possible.

Donna Driver, whose input helped smooth out many rough edges.

Stephanie Stamm, the first reader of an earlier incarnation of this book.

All my blogging friends for their words of encouragement.

Kudos to Glenda Burris and her mad photography skills - how you managed to get a usable shot of such an unphotogenic subject remains a mystery.

Thank you for choosing to read my work, and I hope you enjoyed *Sarah*. I'd be grateful if you could take a few minutes to leave a review at Amazon, Barnes & Noble, or Goodreads.

View other Black Rose Writing titles at www.blackrosewriting.com/books and use promo code PRINT to receive a 20% discount when purchasing.

BLACK ROSE
writing™